CW00859873

G. BAILEY

THE IMMORTAL AND DAMNED

THE EVERLASTING CURSE SERIES

THE IMMORTAL AND DAMNED

THE EVERLASTING CURSE SERIES

G. BAILEY

There is no place for immortal love in the world of the damned.

Vampires. Witches. Sirens and hellcasters.
Can one queen rule them all?
Who will survive when the final war is over?

Riona Dark survived being sold at the auction,
living with two vampire princes, and taking the
magic of the island as her own.
But losing Maddox, the Mad Prince and the
vampire who owns her heart, is too much. The
sirens offer Riona a way to erase her emotions, to
escape the empty pit inside her chest and the

island full of vampires looking to her as their
queen.

But what if it's not the end for Maddox?
Can they save each other before it's too late?

**Warning: This book is a dark romance,
and it contains themes not for the faint of
heart.**

"Staring at the rubble of this building isn't going to bring Maddox back to life or save Riona from the sirens," Katy's cold, piercing voice echoes around me like a fog. I barely breathe as she stops at my side, close enough for her scent to overwhelm me. Ice and berries, that's what she scents like and always has done. But even she, my most trusted guard and a woman I have never wanted far from me, can't dull the sting of this place. The place I watched, powerless to do anything, as hellfire burnt my brother into nothing. Everything after his death is a blur of red and black, including the smashing of the building in Riona's outburst. I woke up under a bunch of brick, the weight of it keeping me buried. But part of me wanted to stay under those rocks forever and never face what happened.

My brother is dead.

My heart cracks in my chest, splintering into pieces. My brother is dead. My little brother, who I was meant to protect. Our mother must be horrified, looking down at just me now. At least he is with her.

Part of me always thought Maddox, the Mad Prince, would live forever and outshine us all one day. When he got his head out of his ass and stopped using his past to define his future. Turned out it took a certain witch/hellcaster to do just that. Riona Dark. For years, Maddox and I argued over everything small and everything big, like the throne. He was never a king until he met her, and for the first time, I realised that maybe he was meant to be the king, with Riona at his side. The pair of them are the perfect mix of light and darkness, and together they shape a future where everything could be free. The vampires love them, the power chose them, and I would bow to them both. But even she couldn't save him from her father.

"She has run away to be with the sirens. That's her choice," I snap back, turning from the rubble of the building my brother died on and back onto the messy street. People are out, cleaning and picking up what is left of the burnt houses in this row. I watch a young vampire woman sweeping ash into a pile, the brush of her straw broom etching on my nerves with each swipe. My fangs ache, reminding me I haven't fed since my brother's death.

It's been two weeks. Fourteen days. Three hundred and thirty-six hours.

It still doesn't feel real. He. Is. Gone.

"Reign," Katy softly murmurs, stepping in front of me this time, capturing my attention as she always has done and never once realised it. Her black hair is cascading down her back, braided away from her perfect and beautiful face. For a second, I remember her in a dress, dancing in my arms with witches all around us on a night not so long ago. It feels a long time ago.

I've never felt much for females other than a burst of desire, easily sated with one long night. I have a feeling one touch, one kiss, from Katy and I'd fall to my knees to beg for a lifetime with her. Something changed between us that night, or at least I had hoped it had, and now there is a coldness between us created by me in my grief. I've pushed her away, and I don't have a single clue how to make a relationship work between us. Part of me wants to run away from her, fight what I'm feeling, but another part of me needs to figure this out because she isn't running away, leaving me to wallow and scream in my pain. I don't deserve her; I don't deserve to be falling in love with her, and I'm powerless to even stop myself thinking of what it would be like to kiss her right at this moment.

I hate that I'm even thinking of her when my brother is a pile of ashes under the rubble of the house behind me.

Katy comes closer and places her hand on my arm, her touch warm. "He would want you to save her."

Fuck, she is right. Maddox would haunt my arse forever if I let the sirens take Riona and warp her soul into something new and heartless. I meet Katy's eyes, not bothering to hide the pain in my own, and she flinches. "I have nothing to show her, nothing to give her. I could save her from the sirens, and then what?"

"I have something."

Katy and I turn to see two of the hellcaster children standing on a flat stone. The girl I recognise from seeing her at Riona's side sometimes, her blonde hair and ember eyes are unforgettable, as she doesn't look like a normal child. A haunted one, perhaps. The other child is a boy, around the same age as the girl.

"Ember, right?" Katy questions. "This isn't a good time, kids."

Ember holds her ground, and not many would have the strength to do that when Katy told them to go. "I am Queen Riona's friend, and I like Prince Maddox, so I asked my friends for help."

She blows out a long breath of air, the only sign she is nervous. "Hellfire can be a portal as much as it can destroy. Prince Maddox is not dead, and we can prove it. If you will let us, your majesty."

I shake my head, a low growl escaping my throat. "This isn't a funny game to play, kids."

Katy places her hand out in front of me and steps forward, watching them. I don't know why she is entertaining this madness. I've never understood children, and now isn't the time to be playing their games. "Prove it then."

Ember turns to the boy and sharply nods. "Show them, Dust."

Who names their kid Dust?

Katy lowers her voice just for me, like she can read my thoughts. "They named themselves. But still."

I turn back as the kids hold hands, making a circle with their arms, and one bright flame flickers to life in the middle of their arms. Slowly, the flame spreads in a circle, washing through the air and creating a flat surface of flame.

Ember turns to me, sweat lining her forehead and her eyes glowing like the fire she has made with Dust. "Quick, come and see him."

Katy moves first, and her gasp when she looks down into the flame makes me move, my feet out of my control, brutal hope wrapping around my heart in a vise. I walk up to the children and look down into the flat flame that shows a world far from here.

What I see changes *everything*.

CHAPTER ONE

My dreams are haunting me.
Punishing me.
Destroying me.

*W*hat is left of my soul, my heart, my core, cracks as I look at a man on his knees, in chains, blood pouring down the muscles in his chest and down his flat stomach before disappearing into the black trousers, mixing with the fabric. His raven black hair is a mess of locks around his head, covering his forehead and touching his eyes. The only colour is the red crystals woven into his hair strands, glittering from the flames outside the cage he is in. The flames almost make the black steel bars of the cage seem red, clashing with the blood covering him.

His eyes have never looked as dark as they do right in this moment. In this dream.

His eyes, that focus on me, like we are really together, are pits of blackness. Pure black, and there isn't any light there like I used to be able to find in the redness.

Red and black, pitted against each other, luring me into their depths.

Now there is only darkness, and it hurts my chest, like someone is physically stabbing me there.

Because this is a dream, and he isn't alive.

Maddox Borealis is dead, and this dream...it's another dagger to my chest.

It's another death for me.

Because I have to wake up.

I gasp as I wake up, clutching the sea blue silk sheets crumpled by my waist and legs, feeling like they are pushing me down. I push them away and crawl off the large bed, stepping onto the cold tiles and letting them shock me back into the real world.

The world without Maddox.

Hot tears fall down my cheeks, following a path marked by so many of them that have fallen before, until they touch my lips. The salty taste only makes me feel numb, like everything does at the moment. I touch my lips for a second, remembering every kiss, every stroke from Maddox like he was just here. I lower my hand, catching a glimpse of the white veins crawling over my fingertips, across my palm. The curse is going to take me to him, eventually. Maybe. Who knows how witch magic works?

I miss him. I need him. I want him back.

But he isn't coming back, and every single time I think about him, I could break apart with how much it hurts. It hurts in my chest, in my soul, and I can't breathe. I gasp for air, choking on sobs as I fall to my knees, wails escaping my lips that echo around the beautiful bedroom. The glass door slides open behind me, and seconds later, cold arms wrap around me and hold me tightly. I push her away and stand up, holding my hand up.

"Th-thank you, but I want to be alone," I remind her. Natalia pauses, rising from the floor, a white dress pooling around her, hanging off her slender shoulders.

Her blue eyes, the very colour of the surrounding ocean, lock onto mine. "They have waited four-teen days to see you, but they will not wait any longer. I tried to give you time, but they wish to meet you and meet the fate all sirens share. There is magic in the sea, and some of our people call her a goddess. She will take all the pain away, transform you and share your power with all our people. We all will be safe, and you will feel free. Finally. Don't you want that?"

"I'm not ready," I say, shaking my head.

She softly smiles at me, walking closer, and I watch her warily. "You called for me. You asked me to take it all away, and I promise it won't hurt in here." She places her hand over my heart. "When you become one of us, you won't feel anything."

Her promise is so alluring, and a massive part of me doesn't even hesitate to want to accept it, to go with her, to have all my emotions taken away and become something new. Something cold and empty.

Natalia isn't those things, not really, but perhaps she could be if she wished, and I need to be like that. The pain from losing Maddox needs to stop. I can't live through this pain.

"Will it stop me seeing him all the time? Seeing his death," I question, my voice cracking and making the whole question seem like a plea. It is, in a way. Being here, on the sirens' island, in their home, is a plea.

For it all to stop. The pain to go away. I need it to go away, into a void, and not to come back.

"Yes," she tells me, her eyes understanding what is so broken inside of me without him here. The only reason I don't tell her yes and leave this room with her, is my brother. My mother.

They are both down in the hellcaster city, with him, and I might be able to save them. I just can't save them when I'm like this, so broken, so crushed.

I look down at my hands and feel the power of the orbs spreading through me, pulling me back to The Onyx.

My home. My city. My world.

But it's all nothing without him.

If I get rid of my emotions, of the pain of losing him, then I can be a better queen. I can be what the people need me to be, and I might be able to go and get my family back. Kill my father.

I meet Natalia's eyes. "Let's go then."

She smiles widely and walks across the windowless room. The only light coming in is from a strange magical light hanging above the bed, glowing colours of blue and green. There is a small wardrobe and a bathroom attached to the room, but I don't know what is outside the glass door. I haven't even looked. I didn't want to leave this room since...well, since I asked Natalia to bring me here to escape everything. I might have killed Reign and Katy in the blast I caused. I likely did, and I can't face that.

I can't face anything, and I'm an utter coward. A coward for a queen. The vampires sure lucked out.

"First, you must change," Natalia says, chatting away like I'm more than a broken doll of a girl. That's all I feel like I am at this point. A doll she can dress if she wishes, because it really doesn't matter.

Nothing does. "This dress will suit your colouring." She looks back at me. "Maybe a quick wash too."

Natalia clicks her fingers, and a whirlwind of water surrounds me, washing me in a warm caress. I close my eyes, feeling my clothes washed away from my body and a dress slid over my shoulders, curling around my neck and tightening around my ribs. The water disappears, leaving me dry as a bone and my hair softly flowing down my shoulders. The dress is a wash of blue layers of satin with a tight corset.

"Perfect, dear friend," she says, hooking her arm in mine and coaxing me to the door. The glass door opens without a touch when we are close to it, and we walk out into a large room with several other doors. I look up at the glass ceilings and realise we are underwater, far under it. The sirens' home is made of glass rooms and tunnels, and outside, there is nothing but crystal-clear sea for as far as I can see.

"Welcome to Lazuli Island," Natalia tells me. "Years ago, before my time, there used to be simply caves, and that is the base of the island, but we have expanded, and now there is all this.

The island is nearly as large as The Onyx, and it goes all the way to the surface in parts. This is the main citadel."

"It's beautiful," I tell her, because it is. Through my pain, I can't help admiring the silver and glass structures, the flowers and water fountains filling the edges of the room. It smells like salt with a floral undertone, and it's soothing for a second. Until the numbness settles back into my chest, into my heart, turning the world cold once more.

Natalia, if she notices any change in me, doesn't comment on it. She rambles on about the various structures, statues, and flowers as we walk through a tunnel and through two other rooms, all of them empty, and it makes me wonder where all her people are. We come to a stop in a room with glass walls, glass ceilings and gold-plated tiled floors that make a circle pattern on the floor. I trace the patterns, noticing they are waves in the sea, as three women walk into the room. They are each as stunning as Natalia, graceful with each step like the sea, and slightly taller than me. Two of them have white hair, eternally beautiful faces, and dark skin covered in white dresses similar to Natalia's.

Ceremony dresses, I realise.

This has all been planned. It was never a question of if I was leaving the room, but a carefully asked demand on Natalia's part.

The clear leader of the sirens has hair the colour of the sea, dark and mysterious, and so much of it that it follows her like a veil across the floor. Her dress is black, but white stones are held in metal around her waist. Like armour. I wonder if she thinks it will protect her from me and the power of the orbs.

"Queen of The Onyx, it is an honour to have you here with us. I sense your power is great," she starts off, no introduction, no asking for my name. Just talk of my power.

I don't need to ask why they want me here then. "My name is Riona, and I haven't been officially crowned queen of anything."

"Yet," she replies with a cool glance at Natalia. "Does she know who I am?"

"No, Andraste," Natalia replies. I hate when people talk over me. My hands glow with power, and everyone steps back from me, even Natalia.

I cool myself down and meet Andraste's cold, empty gaze. She doesn't show a single emotion on her face, because she feels nothing. "Why did you choose to become a siren?"

My question doesn't seem to take her off guard. "Back in my time, a single woman would be stolen from a village and taken on the ship as a good luck charm. And a present to the men, to be shared and used."

Disgust fills my throat, but she doesn't show a single emotion about this, like it's nothing. "I was on the ship for two months before I met Lincoln, a young man who spent time with me and didn't hurt me. He knitted blankets for me, gave me candles and special food to make me pass out while the other men visited. I fell in love with him quickly, but before I could tell him, the captain, a cruel man, noticed. He hung him up like a doll and raped me under his hanging body before throwing me into the ocean."

"Gods above," I whisper in horror.

"I floated for a time, before sinking into the depths. As I drowned, the goddess found me and offered me a new life as a powerful siren, and the pain would end. I took the offer," she tells me. "And then I sank their ship and drowned every man on board slowly, painfully, and I enjoyed it."

"I'm sorry," I tell her.

"As am I that your love is gone. The world is cruel and unforgiving. We take what we want, we kill what we want, and we feel only what we wish. Natalia allows more emotions than a lot of us, but most choose to feel nothing but pleasure," Andraste breathes out. She walks closer to me. "With your power, you could drown the hellcasters' city and enjoy it. You could be anything you want with us, your power shared with us."

Her voice is seductive, luring with every single word. "We would help you in every way you could possibly need. We could share the burden of your power. The pleasure would be unimaginable. Us, together, we could rule the sea and the world."

"We could make sure Maddox is never forgotten," I whisper. "I could get revenge."

"You could," Andraste whispers in my ear, her hands resting on my shoulders. I look down to see a part of the floor slide open, revealing the cold sea below. Water pools into the room, soaking into my slipper-covered feet. It's so cold. "When you're ready, step into the sea and meet our goddess. She will make everything go away, and then we will get revenge. The world will pay for taking your prince."

My dark prince. My Maddox.

This way, I can live on, because I know if I don't do something, I will want to leave this world to be with him.

And if I die, what happens to my family? To Arlo? To The Onyx?

No, I can't let them all down, but I can't continue like this. This is the only way.

"Wait." Natalia steps closer and Andraste hisses at her. She hisses back, and I move away from them both. "It's not the only way to be strong. This is the easy way out, and you won't want revenge after this. You will want nothing and no one. Maddox will be a distant memory, and I don't think that's what you want."

"What are you doing?" Andraste snaps, grabbing Natalia's arm. "The goddess will drown you for this!"

"Don't hurt her," I demand.

Andraste turns on me. "You don't get to tell us what to do while you're not one of us. Become a siren and perhaps I will spare her betraying life."

"Don't do it. I was wrong to bring you here," Natalia tells me, meeting my eyes. "It isn't a good choice, and it's wrong. Maddox would—"

"Maddox isn't here," I breathe out. "He is dead and gone, so who cares what he would have wanted?"

"I do."

Katy's voice makes me jump, and I spin in time to see her step through a portal. Alarms blast around us like a baby screaming, and Katy sighs, pulling out her swords. "I'm afraid you have my queen, and that's a big problem. So no, I'm not leaving."

"You are," Andraste hisses, grabbing my arm. "Or you will die."

Katy rolls her eyes and looks at me as another shadow of a person glows in the portal. "You need to think things through before you act on them, Riona. But don't worry, you're leaving this mistake."

"Why would I?" I ask, tears filling my eyes. "There is nothing left in this world without him. Nothing."

Reign steps out of the portal. "Sister, I think you'll find there is. Maddox is alive."

CHAPTER TWO

"You're lying to make me come back with you, and it will not work," I reply, crossing my arms and holding my ground. I'm glad Reign and Katy are alive, but something cracks deep in my chest when I see Reign, who reminds me so much of Maddox. He is a burning reminder that Maddox is gone. He is gone. Whatever lies Reign is making up are just to trick me, to confuse me, and get their queen back.

But they need to understand, their queen is an empty and broken shell. They shouldn't want her back, not like this. "I know you won't understand, but I am here to fix myself, and then I can be a queen. That's what I need to do. I can't breathe, I can't think straight, I can't exist without him in this world with me."

A sob retches out of my throat, and Reign's eyes lock onto mine. "I'm not a liar, and I wouldn't have come here to stop you unless I was certain. I've seen him and—"

"This is lies!" Andraste shouts, her grip still tight on my arm.

Natalia steps to my other side and looks at Reign. "We are not going to hurt her, Prince Reign. Whatever she chooses."

Reign looks right at Andraste. "Interrupt me again and you won't like what happens."

"Try it, prince," she sneers.

Katy steps in the middle of us and looks at me, her gaze softer than usual, softer than I've ever seen it. The badass warrior vampire feels sorry for me, and I don't like it. "Ember showed us Maddox in the hellcaster city. He's not dead, it was a trick, and I'm certain your father is planning to use it against you. Are you really going to jump into the fucking sea and erase your emotions? Become like them? Your emotions are the worst and the best parts of you."

"I can't believe you," I admit, my voice cracking. "If I believe you and then find out it's a lie, it will destroy me. I'm barely holding on."

Katy takes another step forward, ignoring the hissing coming from Andraste at my side. I barely feel her nails digging into my skin. "I swear he is alive, Riona."

He's alive.

Maddox is alive?

I think back to that moment, the rush of hellfire, the ash, the scream of pain. Some of it was real, but maybe he did trick me. My father could have done that, and I don't know enough about hellfire to know if it only kills. It could have taken him away, to the hellcaster city, away from me.

My father knew it would destroy me to lose Maddox.

Hope, small and painful, trickles into my chest and blooms into a tornado of feelings. And for the first time in weeks, they aren't crushing; they aren't all bad.

G. BAILEY

Katy smiles, seeing the change in my expression before turning to Andraste, her fangs bared. "If you don't let go of my queen, I'm going to rip you to pieces."

Andraste blanches at the threat and very slowly takes her hand off my arm, finger by finger. I spin on her when she takes a step back, and nod my head her way. She nods back, but I can see she is ticking with anger. I sigh and look at Natalia. "Thank you for coming for me."

Natalia inclines her head. "Anytime, your royal highness. I hope our help and willingness to make you one of our own means we can have an alliance in the future."

"We will see," Katy replies, a bite to her tone.

I walk to Natalia and pull her into a hug. Her soft voice whispers into my ear. "I can't see your futures, but if anyone can save him, it's you. Be his queen and show the world what happens when they mess with your king."

Be his queen.

I am his queen, and I am going to save him.

I let go of Natalia first and walk to Reign, Katy stepping in with me. Reign watches me closely as I walk through the open portal, tasting the witch magic thick in the air. I don't know who opened this portal, but it is no doubt another favour The Onyx owes the witches. My people in blood, the same as the hellcasters.

But it is the vampires who have my loyalty.

I step out into the dining room of Maddox's castle. My home. But it feels like an empty shell without him here, and part of me wants to run back to the make-believe world of the sirens and the escape they offer from all this. My power feels like a glowing rock deep within my chest, and being here, it immediately starts to shine, making me feel powerful. The orbs are happy to be home.

The dining room isn't empty at all, and I focus on Ember as she stands and runs to me, wrapping her small arms around my waist. "I'm so happy you're back!"

I embrace her back before lowering myself down to her level. "Is Prince Maddox alive?"

She nods and touches my forehead, opening her mind to me and showing me exactly what I've just asked for. Suddenly a bunch of images jump into my mind, all of them moving too quick to fix onto before coming to a stop.

My heart pangs in my chest as I look at the man through a flat mirror of flames, a portal of some kind. The man is on his knees, blood coating his chest, hair and face, making him look like a monster.

A villain. A monster locked away in a cage.

But I'd know him anywhere. In any world. At any time. Prince Maddox is mine, and he is no monster.

Ember roughly pushes me from her mind, and I stumble back, only to be caught by large hands right before my legs give out from under me. A mixture of shock, hope and joy makes the room spin, and I barely hear the voices in the room or notice who is holding me until he places me down on a chair and kneels in front of me.

Cross McGowan.

My family.

The one who betrayed me.

"What the hell are you doing here?" I demand. He doesn't rise from where he is kneeling, but he looks up, and Reign walks over, placing his hand on my shoulder.

"I asked for their help with a portal in exchange for Tove," Reign explains to me. "Tove was happy to get off the island, and I think she might never talk to any of us again. We didn't make the best impression."

I nod, knowing he had no choice, and I am thankful he came to get me, because Maddox needs me. Maddox is alive.

And I'm going to fight the world until he is at my side once more.

I will kill anyone, destroy anything that gets in my way.

Standing up, the orbs' power pours out of my hands, lighting up the floor around the dining room in a soft red glow. I see Katy moving Ember out of the room as I step right in front of Cross. "I could kill you right now for everything you did. I could level your island with my powers. I could be the villain you painted my Maddox as. I am the same as him."

Cross looks up, and there is terror in his eyes. "Ri—"

"But I won't because we were never the villains. Never, Cross," I firmly tell him. "But I highly suggest you get the hell out of my sight and never come back."

Cross doesn't even blink before standing and running out of the dining room. I look up to Reign, who hasn't moved in the show of power. I like that he knows I would never hurt him.

"Brother," I say, the first time I've ever said that to him. But it's true, he is my family, and he called me sister first, so I don't have to doubt we are on the same page. "I need you to gather every hellcaster child on the island in here."

"Why?" he questions, crossing his arms. I pull my power back, letting it slide back into my body through my arms like liquid red water.

"I want them to practice opening portals to the hellcaster city. Tomorrow, they are going to send me there. Alone," I tell him.

Reign shakes his head. "You're our queen, Riona. I can't let you go there alone. The orbs have been kept out of that world for thousands of years. You can't let your father get them, and he has Maddox there for only one reason: to lure you."

My heart pounds. "I was not asking, Reign. I have to save him, and there is no one else who can do it."

"Not alone," Katy says, walking into the room and stopping at my side. "Reign can build an army here, train the hellcasters, and we can sneak around the city. I will watch your back."

"You could die," I tell her.

Reign shakes his head. "No fucking way."

"I wasn't asking you. It's up to our queen," Katy snaps right back. "And you damn well know she needs someone to go with her. You were just saying that."

"Not you," he growls back at her. I feel like I've missed something between them, because the way they look at each other in this moment only makes me want to run out of the room.

"I'm going to see Arlo and Ann," I say into the silence. "Let me know the choice soon. We leave in the morning."

"It's already been decided," Katy coldly responds, her tone meant for Reign.

"It hasn't," Reign smoothly replies.

On that note, I leave them in their death stare, which I suspect is filled more with sexual tension than anything else, and shut the door behind me in the corridor. The walk past Maddox's room, the memories I have from in there, is harder than I thought. I pause outside the door and go inside, surprised to see the eagle's cage empty, but I know she wouldn't be far from the castle. I walk to the bed and lie down for just a second, breathing in the lingering scent on his pillow. Deep cedarwood with a cinnamon undertone, all Maddox.

Hell, I miss him so much.

"Sniffing pillows now? I'd say it's lame, but I do the same with Austin's," Arlo says, making me jump. With tears filling my eyes, I jump off the bed and meet him halfway across the room, embracing him tightly. He holds me just as tightly and swings me around before putting my feet back down on the ground. "You okay, Ria-banana-llama?"

The nickname I used to hate breaks something in me, and I start crying, pouring out everything I've held back. Arlo simply holds me to his chest, letting me use him for strength until it feels like the wave of sorrow and pain calms. We both go and sit on the edge of Maddox's bed, and I rub my sore eyes.

"My dad is dead. My brother and mum have been taken hostage, along with Maddox. I'm not sure how everything is going to be okay," I admit to him, blurting it all out in a matter of seconds.

"I'm so sorry about your dad, Ria," Arlo quietly replies, picking up my hand and holding it on his knee. "Your dad knew about Austin and me. He walked in on us kissing when we were fifteen, and Austin didn't speak to me for two weeks. Then he started dating Macy Smith. He told me it was to make a point that he wasn't gay and in love with me."

I remember him dating Macy for months. I never liked her.

I stay quiet, listening. "Honestly, it nearly broke me because I was in love with him and confused about who I was. I like both girls and guys, but loving Austin was something else. So for two years, I did what Austin did, dated and fucked everything I could in denial."

"I always thought there was something I didn't know about Austin. A sadness I couldn't understand," I admit.

Arlo nods. "I really did have feelings for you, but it was because you're like him. I'm sorry about that kiss we shared and how confused I made you."

"I get it now," I say. "And part of me wasn't all that shocked about you and Austin."

"Neither was your dad. He picked me up from a game one day, and he took me to McDonald's. We sat there in silence for a while before he looked me dead in the eye and told me not to give up on his idiot ass son, because one day, he is going to realise the love of his life has been there the entire time. I was shocked he didn't judge us, didn't hate us for what he saw. He just accepted it and then said his son was an idiot." He chuckles and I do too. My dad accepted everyone, any size or shape. Austin and Arlo could have joined a flying circus and he wouldn't have blinked.

Tears fill my eyes, and my throat feels tight as Arlo continues, "He was right—your dad always was—and he was like a father to me too."

"He was always right," I mutter, agreeing. "I'm going to save Austin. And my mum and Maddox. I'm going to the hellcaster city tomorrow."

"I want to come," Arlo demands, and I shake my head.

"No. Katy will be coming with me, and that's it. We need to be silent and unseen," I softly tell him. "And you have a baby to think of. You can't die there or get stuck there."

He pauses and blows out a shaky breath. "You're always right, like your dad."

I sadly chuckle, resting my head on his shoulder. "I learnt from the best."

"You're a goddamn queen now," Arlo mutters after a long silence. "A queen of a vampire race."

"It's surreal to me too," I admit.

"He is going to be okay," Arlo tells me, and I don't have to ask who he is talking about. "I won't ever say I like him, but I admire how fiercely he loves you, and no matter what has happened, he will be fighting for you too."

"I hope so," I whisper. "If I lose him, I don't know what will stop me from burning the world down."

He lifts my hand, revealing the curse. "I'm going to search for the missing witch with the vamps that have been sent out. If you'll let me."

"The curse needs to be broken," I agree. "Thank you and good luck."

"Same to you," he replies, and from his tone alone, I can tell he is resting all of his hopes on me. I'm doing the very same.

"When this is over, and my father is dead, I'm going to need advisors. I'd like for you to be one," I tell him. "I can't run this entire island with just Maddox and me making decisions. It shouldn't be that way."

"I like the plan," he replies. "This island is still full of human slaves and poverty that gets overlooked. You can promise them children and a future, and they only have to follow your rules. It's a trade many will take."

"We will figure out a way, but I won't have humans enslaved here any longer," I say. "I was a slave, and now I'm a queen. Fate wove this path for me for a reason."

"Fate's a bitch," Arlo replies, and I laugh, tears falling down my cheeks.

Wait for me, Maddox. I'm coming.

CHAPTER THREE

"Y ou didn't sleep." Ann's kind voice makes me look over my shoulder. I wipe the soil from my fingers and stand up. The sun is barely cresting the city outside, but I know most of the castle didn't sleep well last night. I doubt the vampires in the city did, either. They are sending their queen to hell, and there is nothing they can do about it.

"No," I answer. I feel like I can't rest until I'm in the hellcaster city, until I see him with my own two eyes and make sure he is okay. I don't know why he is in a cage, why he is covered in blood, but I'm sure it has everything to do with my father. Maddox won't be his pet for long. "And I thought I'd clean up the greenhouse, but it seems someone has been doing it for me. It looks great in here, and the roses I planted are blooming."

The greenhouse, which was once a dead and empty shell of a room, is bursting with green life, blooming flowers and vibrant colours. The now clean glass shines different colours across the tiles, and the water fountain fills the silence with a light murmur of running water.

"I did the best I could," she tells me. "I know you're leaving soon. Do you want me to do your hair?"

"Yes, please," I answer. I sit on the edge of the water fountain as Ann works her magic and braids my hair into a plait that falls down my back. My leggings and light grey T-shirt are very casual, but I have the red cloak Maddox made for me hanging on the door. That colour should fit in with the hellcaster city.

Ann walks around me and holds out a dagger in her palm. The blade has been designed with gold to look like flames, and the hilt is a gold crown. "Reign said it was his mother's blade and should be only held by a queen. He asked me to give it to you and make sure it stays hidden until you need to use it."

I pick up the blade, and I think of the red crystals woven into parts of my hair. A present from their family, from an ancestor I can never meet. Ann hands me a leather case, and I slide the dagger back into it before walking to my cloak. I hide the dagger in the inside pocket and slide my cloak over my shoulders, clipping it together.

Ann waits and smiles at me. "Be careful. I know you have to go, but...be careful."

"I will," I tell her. "And thank you for keeping it nice in here. It means a lot."

"You look nervous," she says.

"I am," I reply, blowing out a breath.

She nods. "I would be too."

We don't say anything else, because there isn't anything that can be said, and I leave the green-house with Ann staying behind in it. The castle creaks in the wind, the only sound I can hear as I walk through it and to the library where the hell-caster children are waiting with Reign. The dark circles under his eyes suggest he hasn't slept well either.

"Morning," Reign says. The children are eating off little plates, and I wink at Ember when she looks up.

"Can we talk alone before Katy gets here?" I ask. Reign nods and walks us into the corridor, crossing his arms and looking at me expectedly.

"If I die and don't come back, be a good king and take the vampires away from here. My father will destroy The Onyx out of spite. You can all blend in with the humans, and it will save you all for a little longer," I say.

Reign's stern eyes meet mine. "We won't run, but I am glad to see you thinking of your people."

"I would stay if it weren't for him," I tell him. "I know the risk and what I'm doing."

"I always knew you two would destroy each other. Your kind of love is all-consuming," he replies. "And dangerous to the world."

"And what about you and Katy?" I say.

He skirts the question altogether. "Katy is going with you today. Keep her safe, sister."

"I will try my best, but heaven help anyone that tries to hurt her," I remind him. "I've never known anyone as badass as her."

"Neither have I," he replies, and I tilt my head. "And when she gets back, I'm going to convince her to be my mate."

I'm shocked for a second he admitted this to me, but then I can't help but feel happy for them. So happy for them.

"I knew it," I say with a grin.

"You knew what?" Katy questions, walking down the corridor towards us. I went for casual, and Katy is dressed in red leather, weapons everywhere, a blood red cloak clipped around her shoulders. She looks ready to take down the hell-casters on her own. Suddenly I feel like a sidekick.

"That we are going into hell and it's going to suck," I reply, blurting out something random.

She arches an eyebrow. "Is it time?"

"Yes," Reign answers, giving her one more sweeping look that leaves a blush on her cheeks before walking back to the library. Katy is blushing?

I missed something big between them, and when I knowingly smile at Katy, she glares at me. "Don't ever smile at me like that again."

I laugh. "Sure. Sure."

She glares at me one more time as she walks past, and I try hard to keep the chuckle in my throat before going after her into the library. Reign has seven of the hellcaster children in a circle, one of them being Ember, and he nods us over.

"They want you to stand in the middle, and they will open a portal around you. It might be a bit of a fall," Reign explains, and we both nod.

Ember looks over at me. "There's a woman who owns an inn. She takes in children, and it's where your mother took us. They seemed like friends, and she might help. The inn is called Rockshine."

"Thanks," I tell her. "Be safe here, okay?"

"Okay." She smiles brightly at me. A big part of me really likes Ember, and maybe she could live in the castle and be like a ward of mine or something. I'd like her to have a good life for all the help she has given us in this war. I nod at Katy, and we step in the gap some children make for us. Katy stands close as the children tighten the circle once more.

The air starts to vibrate before five little flames flicker to life around us, one so close to my cloak that I can feel the heat. The flames get bigger and bigger before spreading out in a wave, and then I am falling. I gasp, sucking in hot air, and I barely get a second to open my eyes before I slam harshly into a gravel surface, knocking the air out of my lungs.

I groan in pain and roll onto my back, looking up at the top of the hellcaster city, the flame-covered rock walls.

We are here.

"That looked like it hurt," Katy drones, and I lift my head to see she has effortlessly landed in a crouch.

"It did," I mumble as I stand up and listen to the noise. It's so noisy here; the chatter of people, clashing of doors, and general rumble of an immense city of hundreds of thousands echoes around us as I take in the city. The vision I saw when I took the third orb flashes before my eyes as I look at the castle on the other side of the city, towering above us all like a righteous king. It's exactly where he would live. Right in front of it is a clock tower and a balcony made of black onyx. I remember seeing myself standing there in a silver dress and a crown.

I can't become that version of myself, because I was empty. Katy comes to my side. "We are on top of an enormous building with at least ten floors. Looks like houses, so should be easy to get down to the street and look around for this inn."

I take one more look at the bustling city full of hellcasters and pull up my hood. If we get caught, I can't save anyone. I check on my power like an afterthought, happy to feel it humming with life inside of me.

Not long now, Maddox. Wait for me.

CHAPTER FOUR

The hellcaster city is brutal.

Or at least their people are. Katy and I make our way through a gathered crowd, watching as two hellcasters beat the shit out of each other for sport. I glance through the crowd to the fight as a man slams his flame-covered fist into a woman's cheek, and she bounces onto the dirt floor. She jumps up, her arms thick with corded muscles, and wipes a line of blood off her chin before grinning. I look away as she jumps on the man, with razor-sharp teeth and a show of flames curled around her fists.

Katy looks back at me, her eyes just visible under her cloak, and I nod to tell her I'm okay. The only good thing about the street fighting is no one looks our way as we slide through the crowd and into the streets that have a nasty smell about them. The houses are more like towers, the bricks broken more than not, and all of it barely looks held together. I look up at the black stone tower as we pass it, another housing block. The one we passed down earlier was just as bad as this one, in ruins, dirty and old. Damp and other smells that I don't want to identify linger in the air, and there isn't a breeze to blow it away, it just stays. It's so hot here that my cloak is sticking to me, and sweat trickles down my back. I don't need to see why the hellcasters want to escape this place.

It's not a world. It's a prison.

Katy drops into step next to me, her voice low. We might look alone, but I don't trust any of the deep shadows that could hide someone desperate enough to sell us out. "This place is a maze."

"We need to find a kid and pay them with something to tell us where to go," I suggest. So far, I've seen at least a dozen kids hiding near the buildings, begging anyone that walks past. It hurts my heart to see them, because I see Ember in each one of them, and then I remember my mother saving who she could.

My mum.

It feels like I haven't seen her in forever, and I don't know what to say to her when I do see her. She lied to me for my entire life, but it was to protect me. I need to tell her I understand what she did, and I know it was to give me a chance to escape my father.

I want to tell her I miss dad. That he will always be my dad, no matter what my blood says. I just miss her.

"I will follow your lead," Katy replies and meets my gaze. "Don't get us killed."

I smile at her, and she smiles back, just for a moment, before I get moving. We pass several people on the way to the alleyways behind a large towering building, but none of them even look our way. I get the suspicion that everyone keeps to themselves, or they find themselves in fights like we witnessed on the way here. I would keep my head down if I were them. The longer I spend in this city, the more I realise how much my mum really did protect me. If I were brought up here...

I shiver. I would have been a monster by the time I turned ten.

Katy and I slide into an alleyway and walk to the end where a few large barrels hide a wiggling bundle of tatty blankets and empty glass bottles in a row that clink when the kid moves.

"Come closer and I will burn you," the girl hisses. Katy sighs, sliding her dagger out, and I place my hand on her arm.

I slide off the gold ring on my finger, one I borrowed from the library, and hope it isn't important. I thought it would be a good idea to bring gold to a place like this, in case we needed to buy something. "I have gold. You can take it in exchange for directions."

The girl pops her head out of the blankets, a whip of red hair bouncing around her shoulders. Her eyes are bright like flames under the grime covering every inch of her skin. She holds a knife in her wrapped hands, and I would guess she's about ten.

Too young to be this forgotten.

"Where's your parents?" Katy questions.

"Dead," she coldly replies. "In the king's mines, paying off the debt they had when there was a cave-in."

What the hell is he mining for? Gold? A way out?

She shrugs like it's nothing, but her eyes lock onto the ring with a desperation I hate to see. I want to just give her the ring to save herself from this life she has, but I need to find Maddox. Reign was right, Maddox comes above everything. "That was five years ago. What do you want to find?"

"Sorry about your parents," Katy says. "We are looking for the Rockshine Inn."

She twitches her nose. "Why?"

"A friend lives there," I lie.

"Everyone knows where the Rockshine is. Why don't you? Actually, you look so clean...where are you from in the city? What tower?"

"Do you want the gold or not?" Katy snaps.

The girl laughs. "I bet the king would pay more to find out strangers are in his world."

Katy growls and bares her teeth. The girl doesn't even blink, and she takes a step back. If she runs off and tells the king, we are so screwed.

"I'm the queen of an island called The Onyx, and the king here is my father. He took the man I love, my brother, and mother, and tried to kill me. I'm going to kill him for what he has taken from me, and I'm going to free this city. Including the people in it," I say. Katy sighs in disappointment, but the girl doesn't move, watching me closely. I lower my hood. "My name is Riona Dark, and if you help me, I have a chance of saving you from living like this forever. Isn't that worth more than gold?"

"You're the heir?" she asks, her eyes wide. "The king is looking for you. He is offering a thousand gold coins. A lifetime's money."

Dammit.

"Great, now she is definitely going to sell us out," Katy mutters and slides out another dagger. "I'm sorry, but I'm going to have to stop her. My job is to protect you, and this is a risk. You shouldn't have spoken."

"Don't you dare," I snap at Katy.

The girl looks between us and takes a step forward. "My mother sang songs of an heir who would come and free us all. I don't like the king, and I don't need that much gold. The king doesn't have that many people loyal to him."

"Good to hear. I hate the bastard too," I reply, and she flashes me a toothy grin.

"Come on," she says and nods her head to the end of the alleyway, onto a new street.

Katy catches my arm, her voice low. "I don't trust her."

"We can't trust anyone in this city, but what choice do we have? We won't find this place on our own," I quietly reply. "Let's just—"

A small scream is all I hear before I see the girl burst into flames. Ash rains down onto the dirty ground as my heart lurches and sickness rises in my throat. That poor girl. She didn't have to die. I never even knew her name. A bulk of a man in red royal armour steps through the ash and comes to a stop. There is a crown on his chest in gold, and his helmet is crafted around his large head.

Ten more guards make a line behind him, and I look beyond them to see ten more blocking the exit to our back.

"Did you really think your father wouldn't sense your arrival, Princess Riona?"

Whoever this hellcaster is, he is going to die for touching that girl.

I channel my power into my hands and smile. "It's Queen Riona, actually."

Without pausing, I attack with my powers. Red power razes the ground around us in red magic, shaking it as spheres made of my magic leave my hand, and I throw them at the guards. Three orbs hit the guard who spoke in the chest, and he tries to defend himself only to be thrown back into the others. Katy is on them in a second, swords blazing as she moves so quickly I can't see her. I spin around as the other guards run our way, and I grin, widening my arms. My magic leaks from my body in a wave, and I mentally shape it into a wave before sending it crashing towards them. The wave catches the guards, who try to flee, and burns them into nothing within moments.

I could destroy a whole army without trying.

This world is nothing.

"Stop or he dies." I spin around, my body going deathly still as I lock eyes with Austin. The guard who spoke to me holds a red blade to the neck of my brother, who's breathing heavily, his dark eyes blazing with anger. I barely glance at the guard as I take in my brother and how he looks terrible. Deep bruises mark his face under the dried blood, he is too pale, and I suspect he has taken more than one beating. I'm surprised he is even standing with how bad he looks. Katy lowers the hellcaster in her arms, and he drops to the floor with the pile of others she has taken out.

"Run, Ria!" Austin shouts in a cracked voice, a voice that suggests he has almost lost his voice from something. Something like screaming. The guard laughs.

"She won't."

He is right, I won't, but someone else should give us a chance. I look at Katy and nod. Without looking back at me, she runs past me, and several guards chase her as I put my hands up in the air. We spent hours going over this plan, that if I got caught, then she had to run, find help, and stay hidden. Katy didn't want to leave me, but there was always a big chance my father would know when I was in his world. He would sense my magic, the orbs, returning to the place they were created.

Katy was always plan B. I hope she doesn't get caught, because otherwise we are both screwed.

Gold-plated handcuffs are thrown at my feet, clattering against the ground. They look so out of place on the dirt ground, in an alleyway that smells of filth.

"Put them on, princess," the guard demands, and my magic reacts in my chest, repulsed by the cuffs before I've even touched them. I keep my eyes locked with Austin's as I pick the cuffs up and ignore the way my body instantly feels drained. I click the one around my right wrist, the cold metal nice in the warm heat and click the other one on next. Gritting my teeth, a cold feeling spreads from the metal, up my arms, and settles around my magic.

I instantly feel caged, even as I stand freely on my own.

The guard smirks at me before nodding his head at the guards behind him, and they walk to me. "Put her in the carriage. It's time to see the king."

My feet drag against the floor, and the guards' rough hands dig into my underarms as I'm taken to the carriage and thrown inside. I grit my teeth as the two guards climb in after me, and the door is slammed shut.

"Where is my brother?" I demand, standing up off the floor. One guard slams his hand into my chest and knocks me back into the seat.

"Sit down, princess," he sarcastically suggests, "before I rip your pretty clothes off and see what makes the Mad Prince hard."

"Fuck you," I snap, my cheeks burning. The way he looks me up and down, and his threat make me fear saying anything at all.

He laughs with the other guard, and I scoot away from them both, closer to the window and as far as I can get in the small space. The carriage is dark with the windows covered by thick, gold, tatty curtains, but I can just about see the dark leather seats, dark fabric walls and patterned flooring. The two guards sit on either side of the door to make sure I can't leave, but I don't know why they bother while they've got my brother. There is no chance I'm going anywhere when I saw how little the guards care about his life. They would kill him to make a point, and I highly doubt King Bane would give a shit.

I catch a glimpse of the streets out of a corner of the window near me, where a bit of the curtain is pulled back. Red light pours in, highlighting the cuffs on my wrists. The buildings seem to get taller as we pass them, and less dirty, and I'm going to guess we're going towards that castle that I saw. The one which seems to shine down on the city like a beacon of hope. I don't know what the people have to hope for here. From what I've seen, their king treats them like dirt under his boot. I close my eyes for a second and rest back, remembering that this was the plan and that I'm going towards Maddox.

That's all that really matters.

If I can just find him, just see him, make sure he's alive and well, then we can fix everything else. We always fix everything together.

It's us against the world. He is the other half to my soul, and I don't care what happens in the world as long as he is with me. The cuffs around my wrist jingle with the moving carriage as it goes over what feels like cobblestone, and it reminds me that the cool metal is there. They are some kind of lock down on my power, a darkness within the gold that is lingering. I feel around for my magic, but it's just caged away from me. It feels like it's locked in a darkness that comes from these cuffs. I try to pick at the darkness with my magic from within the cage, and it seems to crack just a little. If I work on it, maybe I can release my magic and break these cuffs.

I am not wearing these things for any longer than necessary, but they will make Bane think I'm powerless.

Perfect for me to catch him off guard.

I think back to the redheaded woman that I spoke to when I got the third orb. The vision of myself so empty and cold, standing on top of that balcony in front of the castle. I can't let myself become that, but I'm scared it's a fate I can't avoid. I'm going down the same path that she warned me of, and I can't become the queen of this place and end up empty. The only reason that might happen is if I lose Maddox.

A sharp pain in my chest nearly makes me whimper, but I push it down. Maddox is not dead.

I just have to find my family. I just have to find him, and then everything will be okay. At least that's a lie that I'm telling myself repeatedly to stay sane. At least I know Katy is safe and I'm not alone in this world. If anyone can sneak around and find a way to get to me, it's Katy.

I can find a way out of this somehow, someway. I'm not sure how, but I'm definitely going to find a way because Maddox and my family need me. The Onyx needs me. The carriage jolts as it goes over something in the road, lifting me off the seat and into the air for a minute before slamming me down. Then it stops quickly and everything is so silent. Too silent. The door is pulled open by another guard, with a silver helmet covering his face, and the two guards in the carriage grab hold of my arms and drag me out. The sweltering heat hits me one more time as I'm dragged across a courtyard and straight through an open door. They move quickly, forcing me to keep up and not giving me a second to look around the place.

The inside of the large castle is pretty similar to what I would expect with its black walls. It reminds me of the castle from the Dracula movies but in all black instead, making it creepier. The walls are made of black onyx that lines the castle, and strange paintings hang on the walls, showing wars, forests, women with crowns, men with crowns, and beautiful beaches. One painting of a dark forest takes my breath away with how excellent it is, and in one corridor, there are paintings of a massive, vibrant city with flames stretching into the sky and people dancing in the street.

I don't know where that city is, but it is familiar. I wonder if it was this city years ago, and this is what is left.

I'm dragged from corridor to corridor and up flights of stairs until we come to the throne room. I don't need to even be told it's a throne room, because right in the centre of the room is a gigantic gold throne with black onyx crystals on either side that stretch to the ceiling. They just shoot up into the air and are shaped into flames. My father is sitting casually on the throne, and kneeling next to him is my mother. Her head is bowed so I can't see her face, but I'd know her anywhere. I can't see her under the silver cloak she wears, only her small hands piled in her lap.

I turn to my father, King Bane, the monster who has ruined everything in his quest for power. He leans against the throne, his hand resting on his bent leg, and he smirks at me like he's the one who has won already when he definitely hasn't.

I sarcastically smile back as I'm dragged through the room and thrown onto my knees in front of the king. He nods at the guards, and they step back, leaving me alone with my father and mother. Not the joyous reunion I wanted, but I'm glad to see her.

While my mum is in silver, my father has a long, dark gold cloak that's littered with black marks that are designed to make symbols. It curls around him on the throne, and his clothes under-neath are quite plain, just dark clothes made from delicate material and large, heavy boots. He has shaved his beard since last time that I saw him, and now he's cleanly shaven and his hair is nicely styled. Everything about him screams perfection as I observe him, like you would do any monster.

I lock my eyes onto his, so black and empty, and I wonder if he was ever good. If he was ever kind or nice or anything other than the power-crazy man he is now.

I see our mum's head twitch slightly, like she's desperate to look my way. But she can't, not when she is at his side. My hands itch to reach out to close the distance between us and throw my arms around her just to see my mum one more time to speak to her.

My eyes catch on the armrest where there is a crown, one I've seen before. I was wearing it in that vision.

It makes it so much more real.

I look away from the crown and the fear it gives me, and back up to my father, who simply watches me closely.

Too close.

G. BAILEY

"Did you come here for your mother, or did you come here for Maddox?" he asks. The question holds so much more power than it seems.

I hate that he doesn't include Austin.

"Both," I reply, making sure to keep my head held high despite the fact I'm on my knees. He laughs, the sound echoing around the empty room, and it is empty. There's nothing else in here but black walls, pitch darkness in each corner, and bright chandeliers hanging from the ceilings. They barely cause much light to shine down on us, but they are pretty, smothered with what looks like thousands of tiny diamonds.

If they have this wealth, it's all for show, because his city is suffering. They need to escape here as much as he wants to with my power. It's something I can play on.

Bane looks down at my mother and puts his hand on top of her head like she's some sort of pet of his. It makes me want to growl; it makes me want to move forward and fight him with everything I have. She's a powerful witch, and here she is, completely subdued by this hellcaster king, someone she once fell in love with.

What made her love him in the first place? What did she see in his darkness?

"Did you hear that?" he asks her. "Our daughter thinks you want to be rescued from me, your mate."

She doesn't reply, like she's a well-trained pet, and I close my eyes for a second to swallow the frustration I feel.

I'd rather die than be a man's pet.

No woman should be owned by a man.

"I thought you killed Maddox," I say, desperate to get his attention off her. "I suppose that was the whole point, to hurt me. To lure me here when I figured it out."

"I assumed he was your mate already," Bane replies, his voice cold. Tense. Empty. "But it seems I was mistaken. If he was your mate, you would have known."

"I have the orbs as you wanted," I reply. "As you planned when you stabbed me. What's next?"

"Why would I tell you, daughter?" he replies with a dark laugh. "You're right, I wanted you here, and I wanted you to have the orbs. All I will say is that you won't survive what I have planned. Your time is limited."

"No!" my mum finally speaks, and he sharply looks down at her. She lifts her head to look at him. "You promised me my children wouldn't be harmed! You can't!"

"Shut up before I make you," he growls back. "Guards!"

My mum looks at me, pushing her cloak back. My heart hurts as I take in her bruised face, the bruises on her neck, and her short blonde hair. Her eyes are so bright but dimmed with sadness, and I want to rush to her.

The guards walk her out, her eyes staying on mine until she is forced out of the door.

"Mothers are always too protective of their babes," Bane sighs. "I never understood it."

"Did you have parents?"

I remember the woman with long red hair in my vision. She said her son stole the throne, and she ran away with the orbs so he couldn't get them.

Bane said a god created the orbs for him.

I'm not sure which story is true. It wouldn't shock me if Bane lied, and I don't know either of them well enough to know who to trust.

"Yes. My mother was immortal, powerful and made the orbs. She was a god of this world," he replies, his voice drifting like he is imagining her. I don't dare tell him I know what she looks like, too. "But she wouldn't share any of her power with me. Those orbs lived within her, and she told me she was given the power to make them by my father. I never met him, but I was his son, so surely the orbs belonged to me?"

"Not if she made them," I respond, and his eyes flash with anger. "The Moral Fall City was hers, and you were the prince then?"

"Yes," he replies. "For hundreds of years until I demanded my throne, my birthright, and she didn't take it well. So I used spells I created to pull the orbs from her body. Little did I know it would kill her slowly. I made a mistake and turned my back on her, holding the orbs, and she struck me."

"Then she ran to The Onyx and gave them to the king," I reply, "knowing you could never get them."

His eyes narrow. "Yes. But look, her plan failed. The orbs are back here, and the same fate is going to happen to you that did her, but this time I will get my orbs."

"So you are going to kill me?" I ask.

"Not yet. The spell has to be done perfectly," he replies, like killing his daughter is nothing. He stands up off his throne and saunters closer. Bane looks down at me for a second before circling around me.

"The orbs will free my people, my army, and I will be the king of every world," he tells me. I knew he was insane, but it turns out he is far crazier than I expected.

"You would murder millions to be crowned king. What is the point?" I ask. "What's the point of being a king that everyone hates? You will be alone forever no matter what crown you have!"

He pauses in front of me and leans down, grabbing my chin. "Don't you want to let our people out into the world? The children who suffer here?"

"No," I bite out. "Not when it would let you out. You should stay here and burn forever."

I should expect it, but I don't, as he hits me hard across the face, and I bounce onto the floor, my cheek burning. Seconds later, he kicks me in my stomach with his large boot, and I gasp, all the air leaving my lungs in a rush of pain. I roll across the floor, a mixture of pain and shock freezing me to the spot. Tasting blood in my mouth, I groan, looking up at the ceiling of chandeliers right before Bane stands over me.

I can see nothing but disgust in his eyes, like he hoped the blood we share would make me as insane as he is. He leans down, and he wraps his large hand around my throat, lifting me into the air. I try not to struggle, but the lack of oxygen makes me after a few seconds, and being this close to him feels wrong.

All I want to do is lift the hidden dagger and stab him in the chest with it, but I suspect only my magic would kill him at this point.

His body flickers in and out; at one point, he is made of blue flames in the shape of a tall man, and the next he is normal again. It's creepy to watch how he changes into a monster, and that is who he is deep down. He has tricked everyone with the face he wears when he is really nothing more than empty fire underneath. I hate that I'm powerless right now.

I hate him so much.

"I can't wait to burn the magic from your soul and watch you die. You might have my blood, but you are not anything," he breathes into my face before he drops me onto the floor. I gasp for air, crawling away from him. I only crawl for a few seconds before two guards are picking me up by my arms and holding me between them.

"You came all this way to see your lover, so you will see him," he says, a sardonic smile on his lips, and he nods at the guards. As they drag me away, he watches with a smirk on his face. Slowly, he whispers three words.

"Meet my monster."

I have no clue what he means, but if he means Maddox, then he's no monster.

Not to me.

CHAPTER SIX

*E*very staircase I'm forced down brings me closer to him. My Maddox. I barely notice the guards' tight grip on my arms, my blood dripping from my swollen and cracked lip, my swelling cheek or the bruises forming on my stomach and the pain that goes with them. The world feels numb, empty, and all there is, is another step towards my Maddox.

As a little girl, I always dreamed about falling in love with a prince, just like Cinderella did. Just like every little girl does.

My prince was the good guy, the saviour of the stories I read and everything my little heart dreamed of.

But in reality, my prince is born from darkness, and part of him will always be the villain. But he would never hurt me, never hurt anyone unless they threatened me. He is the villain I needed to protect me. I'd always choose him, and he is made for me. Our souls are so similar because I was never all good, and part of me came alive when I met Maddox. A darkness I hid deep.

We were shadows chasing the night away long before we met. Maddox embraced his way before we met, and I was ignoring my own. Together, we somehow fixed each other. I saved him and he showed me how to accept both sides of my soul, the good and the bad.

It can't have all been for nothing. We deserve a happy ending, a future, and not to die down here.

The guards push me through a door and into a damp room that has a metallic tang, and it's smothered in darkness. The guards stay by the door, standing still as statues, and neither look at me. I turn back into the darkness, seeing a light ahead, and I walk towards it.

Maddox.

Every breath, every footstep, echoes in the room, but I can only hear my own pulse beating away as I see the outline of a large metal cage with thick iron bars that look like they are plain, with no magic in sight. The light is coming from a small hole in the top of the room, which pours in light from another room with a white ceiling above us. I look back down at the cage as I get close enough to touch the bar and see him.

The world seems to stop. Everything pauses.

Maddox is crouched down in the middle of the cage, his chest bare and his muscles tense as he faces away from me. I run my eyes over his muscular back and up to his dark hair.

"Maddox," I breathe out, hoping he will turn to face me, my heart bursting with so much emotion even as I break apart. He tenses up further than before but doesn't turn, and I search the cage for a door, finding one on the side. I rush to it, needing to be close to him more than anything else. I rush to the cage door and push it open, stepping inside and briefly wondering why the door is open.

Why is he staying in this cage? There isn't much in the cage other than a toilet, sink and a small metal bed that looks bolted to the ground.

I walk around Maddox, hyperaware of every slight movement he makes until I'm in front of him. Seeing him for the first time brings me to my knees, and I almost can't breathe for a moment as he meets my eyes.

And I don't see any of the red, any of the light, only darkness and my own reflection in them.

Maddox looks at me like I'm a stranger, and I don't understand how my father has done this to him in such a short time.

"It's me," I whisper, crawling closer. He doesn't move, his hands held in tight fists on either side of him. I place my hand over his heart, hearing and feeling it race fast. I run my hand up his chest, up his neck, and cup his jaw. "It's Riona. Maddox, I need you."

He moves so quick I barely trace the movement, but one second later his lips are inches from my neck, his hand is gripping the back of my neck, and the other is on my waist. His lips softly, carefully press against my neck, and I close my eyes, a shot of pleasure washing over me from the kiss alone. I can't do much with the handcuffs on, but I want to touch him.

"Riona," he groans against my neck, my name echoing around the room, his deep voice making my body feel weak. I've missed his voice, his scent, and everything about him. His teeth graze my neck, his sharp fangs tearing a line in their path, and I feel my blood welling from the graze. That's when he snaps.

His teeth sink deep into my neck, and I cry out from the sharp pain, right before the pleasure hits. A sweet mix of pleasure courses through me, and I moan as he feeds from me, feeling myself getting wet between my legs. Maddox rips my leggings off and my top next before pulling me on top of his trousers. I reach between us with my cuffed hands and manage to pull out his hard cock, making him growl against my neck.

Never breaking from my neck, he lies me down on the cold ground and thrusts into me in one long glide. He breaks from my neck to push my cuffed hands above my head and hold them there as he bites into my neck again. This time I don't feel any pain, only pleasure.

I kinda like the handcuffs right now.

I moan loudly, the sound echoing as unbelievable pleasure courses through me. Maddox doesn't pause, thrusting in and out of me, fast and hard, every thrust rubbing against my clit. My hard nipples press against his chest, and soon I'm coming hard and fast, and I can't feel anything but sheer pleasure.

"Maddox! Maddox! Maddox!"

His name is like a prayer as he finally breaks away from my neck and roars as he finishes in me, his whole body shaking. Breathlessly, I reach up, rubbing my blood away from his lips as he looks down at me. His eyes change, bleeding back from the darkness and back to the mix of red and black I'm used to.

"Riona," he whispers, a plea, a groan, a mixture of them all. Either way, it breaks something inside me, and I wrap my arms around his neck, pressing my lips to his. I kiss him with all the built-up passion, and he kisses me back with just as much, just as desperately. When I shiver, the room cold despite how hot it is in this world, Maddox pulls away and picks up the cloak. He wraps it around me as he pulls out of me and holds me on his lap.

Maddox searches my eyes, tracing over my cut lip and swollen cheek. "Who the fuck did this?"

His anger makes me shiver. "Bane."

"Dead," he growls. "That fucking bastard signed his death warrant when he stabbed you. I'm going to make it painful for him. It won't be easy or quick."

"I'll help," I reply, and his eyes sparkle with amusement. The Riona he met for the first time wouldn't have ever said that, but I've changed. His world, my world, has changed me.

And I wouldn't go back.

"How are you here?"

"More importantly, what was wrong with you when I came in here? It's like you didn't know me," I question.

He strokes a hand down my cheek. "They put something in the blood, and I black out. I don't know what I do when I'm out, but I'm glad I woke up inside of you."

My cheeks redden, and he chuckles low. "I enjoy seeing you blush."

"You always say such dirty things," I whisper back, and he smiles at me. A guard coughs and I cringe, remembering that they are by the door and likely heard everything.

Maddox glowers at them and turns to look down at me.

His tone changes, the playfulness gone. "Riona, how are you here?"

I can't tell him about Katy, not when the guards are listening and could report anything we say back to Bane. "I came for you. I...I thought you were dead, and it broke me, Maddox. I couldn't breathe, I couldn't exist in a world without you, so I went with Natalia."

His eyes darken. "She took advantage of you at your weakest, and I wasn't there to stop it. I failed you."

I shake my head. "No, Maddox. You didn't fail me. Natalia tried to save her people, and with the orbs in her grasp, it might have made them strong enough to fight my father. I also think she really wanted to help me. Everyone is desperate, and at the end of the day, she didn't have a choice. In the end, she tried to help me leave."

Maddox tilts my chin up, my eyes locking with his. "Even if he had killed me, I would have found a way back to you. I don't give a fuck about death. It's not enough to keep me from you. Nothing is."

"I'd find my way to you too," I whisper, a stray tear falling down my cheek. "I want forever. I want you as my mate. Us, always."

"Always, my Riona," he whispers back, his voice sensual and filled with dark promises. "Now tell me everything that's happened, starting with how long it's been."

For a while, I explain every detail of what happened since the rooftop, leaving out Katy, until we get to seeing my mother.

"Was it hard to see her like that?" Maddox asks. "If I saw my mother at a man's feet, I'd kill him."

"Yes," I say, my voice laced with anger. "She was like a pet to him, and I hate him for it."

"My bloodthirsty little human," he murmurs into my ear. "I've hidden the dagger you had in your cloak. I'm going to get us out of here."

"I thought I was the stabby one," I whisper back.

He grins at me and nods his head to the cuffs. "Now, I like handcuffs, especially in bed, but we need these off."

"I'm working on it," I whisper back. "Trust me."

"I do," he replies. "And let me get us out of here. The timing has to be perfect."

"I won't leave without my mum and Austin," I softly tell him.

"Them too," he replies. "We have to get you back to The Onyx. You're their queen."

"I'm your queen," I correct him. "And you are the only king in the world for me. The Onyx needs you too."

We both pause when we hear footsteps, and I look over to see a guard walking to us. Maddox growls low, the sound echoing and pure frightening. The guard pauses outside the door of the cage, his hand shaking the tray he's holding, before straightening up. He pushes the door open and walks in, placing the tray down.

I freeze when I see it has a silver dress on it and a silver suit with a black bow tie.

The silver dress... It's the one from the vision.

Maddox looks at me, wondering why I've frozen. I couldn't tell him about the vision when Bane could find out about it. Something tells me him knowing I spoke with his mother, my grandmother, wouldn't end well for me.

The guard backs away and steps out of the cage before speaking. "King Bane has demanded your attendance to dine with him this evening. You have an hour, and you must wear these."

"Why don't you leave the cage?" I quietly ask Maddox.

"It's magic," he warns me, his voice laced with a violent edge. He leans closer, his hot breath blowing against my cheek. "But I have a plan. One I've been working on."

"Good," I whisper back. "Let's bring down my father's world and get the hell out of here."

The way Maddox kisses me promises nothing but pure destruction to anyone in our path. The Moral Fall City doesn't know what is coming. Neither does my father.

CHAPTER SEVEN

The silver dress chosen by Bane falls around my body, tight around the waist, held up in an A-line cut at the top, and it's really quite beautiful, made of silk that is the softest I've ever felt.

But I hate it because it's from him. I hate that he is dressing me up like a doll that is meant to fit into his life, his castle, as the perfect princess to be sacrificed.

Because that is what I am to Bane. Nothing but a ticket out of here.

A cold breeze makes my skin prickle, and not for the first time, I wonder how it's cold down here when this whole world is boiling hot outside. It doesn't make much sense, and I feel like I'm missing something.

I'm tempted to pull Maddox's cloak over me, but I decide to leave it on the bed instead and embrace the chill as I know it will be warmer upstairs.

Maddox looks great in his suit, even if he still looks a bit on the wild side. No suit could hide his wild darkness. His hair is still a mess of black waves dotted with the red gems he always wears, and his eyes are like red and black flames, designed to draw you in. His muscular body stretches out the suit, almost making the buttons pop open, and the overall effect makes him look very attractive even if silver is not his colour. I much prefer him in black. I can't say silver is my favourite colour either, and after this, I won't be wearing it. I run my fingers through my hair, which is now a tangled mess of curls that falls to my waist, and it's pointless to try and tame them without a brush. Maddox lifts a curl and wraps it around his finger, his eyes burning with lust. He makes me feel like I'm on fire as he slowly takes in my body in this dress.

"I look forward to ripping that dress off you later," he purrs.

"You can rip it to pieces," I reply, my voice low. We both stare at each other, the room thick with sexual tension, but we can't do anything about it right now. I clear my throat and pull my eyes away. "What do you think tonight's about?"

I look towards the doorway when Maddox's eyes drift over. He doesn't have the answers and they are the only ones that do. I can't see them in the darkness, but I know they are there. The guards change every eight hours; Maddox counted and some of them like to chat. Turns out Bane has told the city the blessed princess has returned to free them all, and he is getting his army ready. The rest of the things they chat about are gossip regarding affairs in the castle and how the king has a new harlot.

Loves my mum? Lying bastard.

Every day spent in this hellhole makes us both itch to get out and do something. Anything. Maddox says he has a plan, and I trust him completely, so I can wait. I know that he'll get us out of here somehow, and then I can do my next part of the plan. The cuffs are tight on my wrists, digging into my skin now, and the magic coming off of them is slowly wearing thin. I don't think it will be long before I break it.

Then everything is going to change. My power is building up, waiting for me, and it can't be caged for long. I just have to break out of its hold before Bane can use the spell that will kill me.

Maddox must notice me focusing on the cuffs, and he seems to know what I'm thinking.

"How long?" Maddox whispers to me.

"Maybe a few more days, possibly a week," I murmur back, and he nods.

"That timing will work for me too," he replies with a dark smile. The city is going to bleed.

I smile back.

Loving the villain has its benefits in more than one way.

I just hope I'm right. I'm only guessing about how long it takes to wind a crack into the magic. It's tiring, and I have to sleep before waking to bite at the magic once more. Maddox puts his arm around my waist as we hear the door open in the distance and the heavy footsteps of many guards.

I'm not surprised to see seven guards outside the cage door, and one of them opens it before stepping back.

They're not stupid, but I do wonder who they fear? The princess that came here willingly and is a ticking time bomb? Or the vampire who can so easily turn into a monster?

I lift my head high and look towards Maddox, trying to remember the fact that I'm not weak and I'm someone that should be feared. I have the three orbs. I'm the rightful queen of The Onyx, and I was born for this.

Maddox is moving us fast out of the cage, with his arm tight around my waist, giving me the strength to stand up. My bare feet scrape against the floor as I walk, and the guards look down at my feet as I go past. I almost smile as they look at each other in a panic, like they probably should have thought about things like slippers or shoes. My shoes were taken, along with my ruined clothes but not my cloak, and I expected them to bring me new shoes to wear. I miss my favourite boots. It makes me smile in some sense to know the guards make mistakes. It's almost humanlike. The horrible thing is, not all the guards in this castle are going to be evil. Some of them are going to be good, but all of them are in our way.

And that means that they're a problem.

This whole city is in our way, and we have to get out of here. It's selfish and cruel, but I won't die in here, and I won't let my father out. He would destroy the world. I have to get out and I have the orbs, though I'm not sure if it's even possible to leave at all. My father can only leave at certain times, and we don't have anyone to open a portal. I'm guessing my orbs might give me a way out on this. I'm hoping they do. They were designed to help him get out of here. Well, that's what he says. Perhaps they could help me instead.

We finally leave our prison and head out into the lush corridors of the castle. The dark walls are eerie, and they seem to hang over us as we walk down the first corridor and to the stairs. Tiny little rocks cut into my feet with every step, making me flinch, and Maddox looks towards me, noticing everything. Without saying a word, he sweeps me into his arms and carries me up the remaining steps. I shake my head with a small smile.

I know there's no point arguing with him to put me down.

"I've always loved carrying you," he whispers, his hand squeezing my ass. I blush and his lips tilt up in amusement.

One of the guards coughs, and I miss what he says, but Maddox doesn't. One minute I'm in Maddox's arms, the next I'm standing on the carpet at the top of the stairs, and Maddox is holding the guard against the wall by his throat.

"You made a mistake talking shit about my queen," Maddox states, his voice dark and empty of any humanity.

He snaps the guard's neck and lets his body drop to the floor. The other guards all step back, their swords out and flames curling around their hands. Maddox straightens his suit and smiles at them.

"We best get moving," he suggests, a touch of promised violence to his voice. "We wouldn't want to be late?"

The guards look between each other as Maddox steps back to my side and winks at me. I shake my head and try not to look at the dead hellcaster guard.

The guards move into place and keep a tight circle around us as we carry on down the corridor, but this time they are all tense, watching Maddox carefully.

I smile. They couldn't stop him if they tried.

Maddox stays right at my side during the entire walk into warmer parts of the castle. This part of the castle is almost brighter too. Big diamond chandeliers hang all the way down the corridor, and they light up the onyx walls, almost making them shiny. The floor is carpeted in a deep red, luscious velvet, and it's quite nice to walk on. There are several little side tables filled with fresh flowers that are magical. They are flowers I've not seen before, and I'm fascinated by them. They're mixes of red and orange, almost lit up at the ends, with tiny little sparks of embers flying off them but not burning anything they land on.

I want to ask what the flowers are, but after what just happened, I doubt they would tell me. We turn around a corner and come to a big open space. In the middle of the room is a long dining table. The table is made of pure glass, but it's not any kind of normal glass. Fire snakes up and down inside the glass, softly changing into swirls and patterns like it's alive. More of those flowers make the centre-piece, but these are larger, spreading up into the air like a tree and sparking little red embers every-where on the table. They don't set the red place-mats or glasses alight, they just disappear. The table is empty of food and guests, and there are red velvet chairs pushed up against the table, each place setting already laid out, ready for guests.

"You have to sit down," a nervous sounding guard suggests. Maddox gives him a look that would make any man back down and rush away before he walks me across the room.

We sit down at the table next to each other, and I move my seat a little closer to his.

Maddox leans across and brushes some of my hair away from my ear, sending shivers down my spine.

"I've memorised every single one of these guards' faces, and I'm going to rip every single one of their throats out," he informs me. "No one gets to look at you."

I don't doubt it. And at this point, I probably wouldn't stop him, as the guards aren't respectful and they seem like pure assholes.

I lean my head on his shoulder as we wait. And wait. And wait. Eventually I hear footsteps behind us, and I turn to see Bane walking in, and on his arm is my mother. She looks beautiful in a long silver dress, one that's similar to mine, but hers is more detailed, filled with lace and frilly parts. It's funny because it's something she would never wear. I don't think I've seen my mum in a dress like this ever. She's always the one who wore leggings and large hoodies and her hair up in a messy bun. A normal mum. The woman in front of me is a complete, utter stranger in that sense until I meet her eyes and see the same warmness there that always was.

I miss her, even when we are this close. There might as well be miles between us. Her eyes flicker to Maddox, and I swear I see relief in them.

I look behind her as Austin walks in, two guards stopping at the door, who must have been his escort. I wonder where he is locked up. Austin's in the same matching silver suit as Maddox, his face still littered with bruises, some of them fresh. His lip is cut in two new places, and I nearly gasp when I see his ear is missing, nothing but a bloody mess left. I don't need to know who did that.

I look at my father and glare at him to make sure he sees the look of disgust and horror on my face.

I hate what he has done to Austin, and what he is still doing to all of us. I don't want to be at this meal, pretending to play happy family.

My mother sits down opposite me, right next to where Bane sits down in his gold suit. I'm sure it's to make a point that he wears gold while all of us are in silver, a lesser metal to his. I hate all the passive-aggressive, unspoken things that are going on in this room.

Austin sits down next to Maddox and looks across at me. He's saying a million questions in his eyes.

Are you okay?

Why did you come here?

Is Arlo alive?

You shouldn't have come here at all. The last isn't a question, but a statement. I don't need to tell him why I came here. He should know. I have to look away because it's overwhelming, and I find Bane's eyes looking at us with a knowing smile that I want to wipe off his face.

"I'm so glad we finally had this family meal, even with you here, Maddox," Bane states, folding his hands together in front of him. "Though I was happily shocked to find that you weren't my daughter's mate yet. Maybe she will wake up from her infatuation with a monster soon enough."

No one says a word, and Bane sighs. "Unless you managed to fix that mating issue. My guards told me they had quite a bit of a viewing earlier this week."

"Shut the fuck up," Maddox growls.

"You touch me or anyone at this table, and then a hundred guards would be here in an instant, and you'll watch as I kill her," Bane replies, gesturing towards me. "One way or the other, she dies. I'd much prefer she dies in my own timing, releasing all the people in the city, but I would kill her to stop you."

"You'd need more than a hundred guards, Bane," Maddox replies. Only because I know Maddox well do I see under the facade he puts up, and I see the worry for me under it. He couldn't fight them all and protect me.

And I can't fight with my magic while I have these cuffs on. I look towards Maddox and slowly shake my head. He sits back, and I take that as confirmation that he's not going to jump across this table and attack Bane. Not yet.

Bane smirks in victory and claps his hands twice. The room is soon filled with waiters who place various plates of food on our table and bring a large glass of blood for Maddox. After that, fourteen women come into the room, of all ages, but the one thing in common is their beauty. They're all dressed like belly dancers, with skirts of thin orange chiffon and matching bras. They have high heels on that would trip me up in a second, but I can't help admire them. They all have bells and coins attached to their skirts that jingle as they walk.

I watch as they place themselves in different spots around the room, and slowly music starts to play. It's a familiar song, twisted and changed to be more upbeat, and I like it. The dancers immediately start to dance like controlled puppets, perfectly in time and not a footstep out of place. Slowly, their bodies start to light up with fire as they dance, embers flying out of their hands that make a circle around them. Several circles are created around their bodies, and those flames dance with the women. It's rather mesmerising to watch the flames, the dancing, the skill it must take to hold that magic continuously. They never once blink or look away or show any emotion, and it's really quite fascinating.

"My dancers, everyone. Aren't they magnificent?" Bane says, watching them, and the flames reflect in his black eyes. "Each one of these women was hand-picked for me as teenagers. They dance until they break or burn."

I try not to imagine that ending for any of them.

I don't answer. I don't scream at him like I want to. I've got to play nice for now. He already knows I hate him, and that isn't going to change. But he doesn't need to know my plans for what's coming next. I have to get through this meal. Get through all of this.

"I have a deal for you, Riona," Bane states, looking directly at me. Mum looks between all of us, a tiny moment for her, but I notice it. Her hand clutches tightly around the knife in her hand. Bane briefly glances at her and smiles as she carries on eating, before turning back to me.

"Deal?" I echo.

"Yes, there's a game that all royals in our family can play. It was created thousands of years ago, and I played it once," he explains. "So did my mother and her mother and so on. I wanted Austin to play the game, but he is too weak."

"I disagree," I reply quickly and without thinking.

"You would, being his twin," he responds. "You're blinded to his weakness."

I try really hard not to roll my eyes.

Maddox places his hand on my knee, moving closer, his whole body tense, ready for the attack. "Will you play the game?" Bane asks, looking at me intently. "And in exchange, I'll give you something."

"What kind of thing?"

"One request," he answers. "One thing, but it can't be escaping from here. I don't have that power, but something else."

Maddox looks down at me, and I meet his gaze. I'm not being asked to play. This isn't a question, it's a demand and another game. He wants to see if I will refuse, but I don't doubt for a second the game isn't already being set up in my name.

I nod and Bane grins.

The rest of the meal is tense and quiet, but it's better than hearing Bane go on and on. The only sound is dancers and the music, which switches tunes now and then. Eventually, the meal ends when Bane and Mum have eaten everything. Maddox, Austin and I haven't touched anything. I've just moved the food around, not trusting Bane not to drug our food.

Bane stands first and steps over to pull my mum's seat out. I stand up and Maddox moves to my side quicker than I can track.

I want to get the hell out of here, even if it means going back to the prison. As I pass Austin, his hand reaches out, and he brushes my fingers just a little. A sign of comfort. Everything in me wants to rush and give him a hug.

I hope he knows I'm going to fight. I'm going to win and get us out of here.

"Oh, by the way," Bane calls, and I look up at Maddox, whose jaw tightens as we both turn. But he isn't looking at us. He looks towards the door as it opens. All the guards that escorted us out here are waiting outside.

Bane clicks his fingers, and they burst into flames. I turn away as the guards scream and scream until there is silence.

"They should have brought you shoes," Bane says as he walks past me and through the piles of ash, all that is left of the guards, even as new guards come rushing over.

Maddox looks down at me, and I know we are thinking the same thing. How do we fight powers like that?

How do we take down the insane king?

CHAPTER EIGHT

I stare up at the hole in the ceiling, which is some sort of metal grating, and it pours in the only light in this room right onto us. I wonder if it was a viewing room of some sort years ago, and then I wonder if it means my grandmother was all good if she had a place like this. I curl up on Maddox's chest, and he grumbles a little in his sleep before pulling me even closer, burying his head into my neck as he moves down the bed. I run my hands down his back to comfort him, as he needs this sleep. It's been three days since the meal, and I'm hungry, tired, and grumpy. Maddox is worse. He refuses to feed from me, claiming I need my strength, and he didn't want to sleep in case someone came in here and took me.

It took a while, but he finally gave into the need for sleep…but I wish he would feed on me. I'm already weak, and there isn't any point in both of us suffering.

I think back to my mum and Austin at the meal, and everything that happened. How I wish I could do anything more than be forced back into this cage. I sigh and carry on wearing down the barrier of darkness around my magic, making tiny crack after tiny crack until it finally breaks.

And it will break.

I hear the door opening a second before Maddox is awake and pushing me back on the bed as he stands, fangs out and bared, ready to attack anyone who comes close. I sit up and watch as a figure slowly comes into view until I can make out it's a woman.

A very familiar one.

I have to keep my features neutral and give nothing away as Katy comes into view, carrying a plate with a bottle of blood and food for me. Maddox looks down at me, and I softly shake my head to warn him not to say a word. His eyes narrow, but he doesn't say a word as I stand and Katy comes to the cage door and pushes it open. She places the tray down and pushes back her red hair, which must be a wig, and meets my eyes with her green ones. I'm guessing contact lenses, but I haven't a clue how she managed all that down here.

She winks at me before walking away, and I watch her go before Maddox goes to the tray. He carries it back to the bed and places it between us.

"Secrets?" he asks, the single word hanging between us.

"So many ears around here," I gently explain without giving anything away. I lift the plate, not surprised to see a note underneath. I read the note without lifting it, pretending to look through the various breads, cheese, and grapes.

"I'm here and ready. The food is safe, and be careful. The king won't let you win tomorrow. It's all set up."

"Dammit," I mutter under my breath before carefully pulling the note out and sliding it into my cloak pocket. I look up at Maddox, who is tense and staring at the bottle of blood like it's his own personal enemy.

"It's okay," I tell him.

"Every drop of blood I've touched here made me forget. I could have done anything in that time, and I wouldn't have known," he reminds me, but I haven't forgotten. It's horrible what happened to him, and I hate to think what happened when he wasn't aware. The sex we had flashes into my mind. How out of it he was. I don't think he knew who I was, not fully, and it was only our connection that brought him back.

Whatever drug it was had made him uncontrollable, like a caged monster, just like my father said.

I hate him so much.

"Trust me," I ask, lifting the bottle and uncapping it. I hope it's animal blood, and I try not to think about it too much as I pass him it. He gulps, his eyes flashing like fire for a second before he takes it.

I open the water bottle and take a long drink before digging into the food. Maddox has drunk all the blood in moments, and he wipes his lips and waits for something. After a few minutes, he puts the bottle down and watches me as I eat my food.

"I will be strong enough for you to feed on me," I say with a coy smile.

His lips twitch with amusement, and his voice drops. "I think you just like having me inside you. In every. Single. Way."

My cheeks burn red as he laughs, and I love hearing his laugh, how normal it is between us. For a moment, we can pretend we aren't locked up in a world that isn't our world, and my life isn't literally a ticking time bomb. My eyes betray me as I flicker a glance to my arm, the white veins crawling all over it.

The Mad Prince loves me.

And I will pay the price of the curse a million times over.

"I will save you if it's the last thing I do, Riona," Maddox vows. "You will not die from that curse."

"I know," I reply, and he arches an eyebrow. "Arlo is going to find the witch, and I trust him. Your job is to get us out of here and spend forever at my side."

"Arlo?" he questions, pulling a face. "Maybe it was a good thing I didn't kill him after all."

"Yes, it was," I deadpan.

Maddox simply smiles. "If he ever looks at you like you're more than a friend, I will end him, though. Only I get to look at you that way."

I shake my head, secretly loving his possessive nature. It does things for me. "Does it matter when I'm only ever looking at you?"

He leans across and kisses me, a sharp metallic taste lingering in my mouth when he moves back. "Yes. You're mine."

"Tell me something you want to do when you're out of here," I ask, running my hand over his chest.

"Very naughty things, Riona," he replies, and I pat him.

"I mean like go to Paris," I suggest.

"Why Paris?" he asks me. "Is that where you want to go?"

I sigh, thinking on it. "No, I want to go to Greece and sit on a beach with you and pretend to be humans. I want us to be forgettable and mix in with all the tourists. Then it will just be us."

"I doubt very much you would be forgettable to any male," he tells me. "But we will do this. A beach, in Greece, naked—"

"I never said naked," I interrupt, and he smirks at me.

"It's the way I see it," he tells me. I bet. Laughing, I cuddle him tighter, imagining the beach, the hot sand, and the even hotter man at my side. We could go anywhere in the world, travel together and see everything.

He is my home, and we will have a future out of here. I won't ever give up on us.

CHAPTER NINE

*S*oft, billowing clouds surround me in a comforting embrace, and yet all *I* can focus on is her long red hair, which drops in between the clouds, disappearing below. The red is a stark contrast to the white clouds, and it's so out of place. I stand on the clouds, in a white dress that whisks around my legs in the wind. Yet the wind doesn't move her hair at all or the silver dress she wears. She just lies there, looking up at the cold ceiling of the room. I'm quite aware that a room shouldn't have clouds as a floor, wood walls and the cement ceiling. It doesn't take me long to figure out this is a dream or vision or whatever it is where she comes to me.

"You never told me that you're my grandmother, only that we are related," I say, speaking for the first time. I didn't

ever expect to see her again, but something makes me happy to have this time with her.

"Well, titles do not matter much when we will never meet outside of here and I'm long dead," she replies. "I can only come to you one more time. I was given three times."

"Who gave you that?"

"Do you really believe you're alone in this world, Riona? That you aren't being watched, guided and protected by the unknown? There is much you will never know until it is your time, and that's how it should be," she softly explains. "But know you are never alone."

I've felt alone so many times in my life, and if someone is guiding me, they aren't doing the best job so far. Everything is seriously messed up. My grandmother really is beautiful and enchanting in an otherworldly kind of way. I stare at her for a second, wondering if I have any of her looks. I see some of it, I suppose. Maybe, but not a lot. I find my mother's side too much, but I don't count that as a bad thing.

"What's your name? You never told me," I question.

"It's best you do not know it, Riona," she replies. In case I accidentally say it in front of him. "Riona, your fate is

linked to another, and if you take what is right in front of you, you will be free."

"What does that mean?" I ask.

"Oh Riona, I cannot tell you. You must make the decision on your own," she whispers to me, her voice easily carrying to my ears over the small space. "But you will survive what is to come. It will not break you. You've been broken far worse, and I know you can survive this."

"Whatever he throws at me, I will not break under his hand," I say. As long as I have Maddox, I can fight the world.

"I know this," she replies, standing up. "But some things, some things are a test of the soul."

Her red hair is like a curtain around her back, and it really is beautiful. Almost looks like it's laced with gold. She walks to me and gently places her hand on my shoulder and leans in. She whispers something in my ear, and it changes so much.

It changes everything.

The dream is fading as she leans back and smiles at me, both of us keeping a secret.

Secrets hidden in dreams.

I wake up slowly in the prison room, looking up at the cage bars above me and above that, the grating and the light pouring in from the other room. Sometimes I swear I hear footsteps in there, but I can't see anyone. I think back to the dream vision, whatever it is, and something relaxes inside me, knowing that I have one more time to see her. To say goodbye. To thank her for giving me the orbs and for sacrificing her life to get them away from him. I'm just glad at this point. A grunting catches my attention, and I look up as Maddox pulls himself up on the bars with just his hands, his feet leaving the ground.

Sweat slides down his back as he does his pull-ups. It's quite the view to wake up to, and I'm completely in awe watching.

And a little turned on. Okay, more than a little. He really has an amazing body, and he is so beautiful. I don't think I've seen anyone as muscular as he is. He looks back at me and drops to the floor, wiping his hair out of his face. I smile at him as he leans over me, popping a kiss on my forehead before going to the sink. He washes his face and neck and back with cold water before drying with the small rough towel that they gave us.

"Sleep well?" he asks me.

"Something like that," I tightly reply, wishing that I could tell him exactly who I saw in my dreams. But I feel like it's not safe to talk about her anywhere in this castle. There are too many ears, and I know our conversations are being listened to, then repeated back to Bane.

"I wouldn't be surprised if the test is today," I say. I just have a feeling it is.

"I hate this," he replies with a tight jaw. "I wish I could do this for you and take your place. I don't like it, and I'm not going to let them easily take you from me."

"I know," I say, sitting up. I pull my knees to my chest and wrap my arms around them as he paces the cage.

He wants to burn this world down for me.

And funny enough, I have the power to do just that, but I'm cuffed.

I watch him as he stalks over to me. "If it didn't cost you your brother and mother, I'd destroy everyone in this castle."

"But you can't," I softly say, knowing this is breaking him inside as much as it is me. His eyes flicker, like flames going out in a dark room. He hides it well, but I know he is struggling in more than one way. "You're hungry, Maddox."

He smiles and brushes some curls away from my cheek. "Always, but only for you."

He won't drink what they give us, and I don't blame him. The food seems fine for me, at least. I was reluctant to eat any of it when it wasn't brought by Katy, but my hunger gave out in the end. I nibbled on some of the bread, and so far, there haven't been any effects.

I yawn and try to hide it behind my hand. I'm exhausted, even after sleeping, but I have to keep biting away at the binds on my magic. I know I'm close, I can feel it, but it seems harder every single time.

"I can get us out of this. I know I can," I say, lifting my hand up to him, offering him my wrist. "But you need to feed."

"No," he says, taking my hand and holding it in his. "I love you for offering."

"I'm worried, Maddox," I say.

"Do not worry about me being a bit hungrier than usual. It only makes me more dangerous," he replies with a dark smile. He has a fair point, and he has won this argument. I don't say anything out loud as I crawl into his lap. I place my head on his shoulder, wrapping my arms around his waist. He embraces me back, and we just sit there for a moment in silence. Content silence, even in this horrible place.

"Don't fight them when they come for me," I ask him softly. "They could tell Bane, and he would hurt my family. They could force you to have that drug stuff, and I don't want that."

"I've never felt so powerless," he admits.

"I know this is hard, and I don't want to be away from you," I gently reply. "You have to trust me to look after myself for a while. He won't kill me."

"There are far worse things to do to someone than kill them," he tells me, his eyes flashing with memories of probably things he's done to people that are far worse than killing. I try not to think of it or what's coming up for me next.

"I love you, Maddox," I say. "Your past and all."

"And I've never once deserved you," he replies. "But I will never, ever love anyone like I do you."

He leans in and kisses me softly, gently. The kiss soon turns from soft and gentle into passionate and deep. His tongue slides into my mouth, battling with my own, and his hands glide into my hair, holding tightly. I moan into his mouth, and that's when he pulls away, leaving me wanting more.

"I don't want the guards hearing a single moan like that from your lips," he murmurs. "Those are for me alone."

He leans closer, running his thumb across my lip. "I can't wait to get you alone and take you as my mate."

A shiver shakes through me at the thought. We don't get more than a second to talk about mating before I hear the door opening. Some part of me is relieved that this test is finally here, that there's no more waiting, but most of me is nervous. Maddox helps me stand and clasps my hand as I try to count the many footsteps coming towards us. Eventually, I see four guards. Maddox growls low as I take a step towards them, and one of them opens the cage door. I lean up and kiss him softly once to say goodbye without saying that word.

"Hurry back," he urges. "And don't you dare let him win."

"Never," I reply. "My lover taught me how to be fierce. He taught me how to be a queen that doesn't give in."

"I like the sound of him," Maddox replies, and I chuckle as I let go of him.

I walk out of the cage to the guards, who stand around me, and we walk to the door. I step out into the corridor after one of the guards, my bare feet already getting cuts from the rocks that litter the floor. One of the guards stops me and offers me a pair of shoes. They are small black leather shoes, and they look about the right size. I can't see his eyes under the helmet, but there's a silver symbol on his chest that suggests he's different from the other guards in some kind of rank.

"Here," he gruffly says.

"Thank you," I reply as I take them, and I pause. I might be stupid for saying anything, but I need to say it. "I didn't tell my father, by the way, about the shoes. I never would have wanted all those guards dead over a goddamn pair of shoes. It was wrong, and I am sorry for his actions. I wish I could have stopped it."

The guard doesn't say anything, simply stepping back. I slide the shoes on, and as we start to walk, the guard lowers his voice. "We know, princess." His tone is almost kind and completely unexpected.

I look up at the steps before starting to ascend them, wondering what kind of fresh hell is waiting for me in a test for royals.

CHAPTER TEN

The air is thick and uncomfortably hot as we walk through the castle, down the familiar corridors, and I try to mark a path for myself, but it's a maze. We come outside to a balcony and walk down several flights of stairs, out where the walls are so high I can't see anything else, but the fresh, albeit warm, air is a welcome relief. I missed being outside. The guard in front of me blocks the view for only a second before I see the massive gardens filled with flowers. The flowers are huge and thick, stretching to make forests of them on either side of a large clearing with a dip in the middle. The flowers flicker embers all around us, and they look like falling stars, bright and beautiful.

Right at the front of the gardens are Bane and Austin. Austin is wearing cuffs, smothered in his blood as they cut into his wrists, but he doesn't move. I don't see any new bruises on his face, and the cuts look better than before. He looks up like he can sense me, and I try to give him a reassuring smile. I instantly don't like that my brother is here, but I feel powerless to do anything.

As the guards step back, I walk straight up to my father, and he pointedly looks down at my shoes before meeting my gaze. His expression gives nothing away, but I can see how happy he is. He's planned this for years; he must have done. Ever since my mother left him, ever since he knew we were born, it's probably been an ongoing plan. All this time, as he's desperate to get these orbs back and us. He seems like a completely sick bastard to do this kind of thing, because it's all about control. He needs to control everything around him, and while we weren't at his side or at his feet bowing, we weren't under his control. Truthfully, he most likely hates us for taking our mum from him, because she would always choose us.

"My children," he says eventually. Of course he had to start with a really pompous attitude. God, I hate him. "I'm really looking forward to today. It gets boring down here."

"I can imagine," I reply dryly.

"You can walk straight through my gardens, and you'll find the test begins there. It's easy, really. You can bring one person alive out of there, just one. That's it. The rest are sacrifices," he says with a cold smirk.

"One?" I ask.

"Yes, the right person," he says with a small smile. It sounds like there are going to be more people in this test than I thought. Is that why Austin is here? Is he one of them? Where is my mum? I look towards Austin and back to my father. "Oh yes, I brought him here to watch. Won't be fair to have his sister risk her life without having her twin brother there to watch. It might teach him something about strength to see you go through this."

I pause. "Did you ever love us? You know, we're actually your children, right?" I ask. "You claim to love our mother, that she's your mate, and we are children of that mating. Yet you do this to us. This isn't how you love someone. Do you even know how to love someone? Was it because your mother never loved you?"

He looks down at me with cold contempt, and before I can blink, he whacks me really hard across the face. I stumble a little, but I don't fall this time, having gotten used to him hitting me. He certainly isn't winning any parenting awards. I straighten my back and try not to flinch at the pain throbbing in my cheek.

I got my answer, though. His reaction said it all.

"You don't get to speak to me like that. I am your father," he angrily snaps. "Now go and play the test before I decide to make you pay for speaking out of line."

"Yes, Bane," I reply sharply. I look once more towards Austin. His eyes search mine.

"Good luck, sister," he tells me, his voice broken and cracked, sounding like he's been screaming too much. It hurts my heart to hear it, and it makes it ever so hard to walk away from him when all I want to do is destroy the monster hurting my brother. The cuffs remind me they are there, jingling as I walk away through the garden.

I never wanted the power of the orbs, the strong magic and responsibility that came with it, but now I can't use the magic to save my family, my man, and my people. I realise I always needed it. The magic was always mine.

I walk through the garden until I can't see my father or Austin over the hill. I go deeper and deeper down until I come to the bottom of a crater the size of a football pitch. There's really nothing here, just a stretch of dirt, and I can't even see above the hill on the other side. It's too high. I look around, a frown on my face, wondering what the hell I'm going to be doing. Ever so slowly, the ground starts to shake, and I brace myself. A scream is ripped out of my throat as a piece of earth shoots up in the sky in front of me. The ground under my feet shakes before it does the same, and I'm thrown up in the air as I dig my fingers into the dirt to hold on. I clutch the ground as tightly as I can as it stops, jolting me up in the air once. I stand up on shaky legs as the ground around me starts to rise in all different pointed levels.

Dozens of towers of raised earth appear, and the height makes me dizzy. It doesn't take me long to see where the people are, right ahead of me, and it's worse than I thought. Just outside the crater are five people tied to wooden pyres. One of them is a young child with short black hair and dark skin, dressed in a pretty silver dress. My gut feels like it's been punched as I look at the young girl, who can only be about ten. She's tied in the middle, and a woman next to her is trying to reach to her, wriggling in her rope, and she has long black hair and similar features to the girl. I'm going to guess that she's her mother. The others are all men, and all of them look unconscious. I look around, wondering what I'm meant to do before making a bad plan.

I'm going to just jump across the raised earth to get to them, and I can only take one of them back.

But why would this be dangerous? It all seems too easy, and I don't like it. Seconds later, something else bursts out of the ground in a blast, and I duck as dirt rains down on me. Dirt with embers in it. I look down to see what looks like a massive bird, but it's made of pure fire with a long tail and long beak. It squawks loud, and the sound burns my ears. Soon after, dozens of the fire birds fly out of the hole, all of them smaller than the big one, but there are so many of them. They follow the big fire bird, swirling around the raised earth like a wave of fire. My god, they're going to burn the people.

That little girl.

No. Hell no. It's not happening.

Without thinking, I jump onto the next ledge of earth right in front of me. My cuffed hands make it hard to grab onto anything, and I nearly fall. I use my knees to pull myself up, grazing them against the dirt before standing. The flying birds are getting higher, crawling with every wave, and I regret looking at them. I jump to the next ledge and the next one, which is easy, and I don't have to even fall to my knees as I manage to stand. I keep jumping until I'm covered in dirt and getting close. The girl and her mum have noticed me now, and they both look terrified. I'm only halfway across the crater when the fire bird rises up right in front of me. I jump back as flames bounce off my hands, and I flinch in pain. I was wrong, the fire birds are more phoenixes up close, and they're beautifully deadly.

Maddox would like them. The sharp beaks and the red eyes make them look ever so dangerous, and I know they must be. They swirl around me on the ledge, right below me, and I don't think they know I'm here. I look down at my fingers and see there are welts on them. I don't think I've ever been burnt. These phoenixes aren't normal, and that isn't hellfire. The girl starts crying, and it makes me stand, pushing away the shock. The major problem I've got is the next ledge means I need to jump over these phoenixes and the path that they're making.

The flames flicker up in the gap, and I know it's going to hurt. I take in a deep breath of air before running and jumping. I feel my feet catch on one of the bird's wings, burning me before I slam hard into the ledge on the other side. It takes the wind out of my lungs, and everything hurts as I roll onto my back, pulling my feet towards me. They're covered in little burns, blistering and bleeding already, and it kills me when I stand on my feet.

I must get to the girl. Nothing else matters right now. It's just pain. I look towards the next ledge and realise I can make three more jumps. I could get right in front of them. I run and jump onto the next one, everything hurting me as I do. But I'm ahead of the phoenixes now, just by a little. I have to keep moving. I don't pause as I jump to the next one and the next, and then I'm right in front of the pyres. I'm not sure how to get onto that last ledge, but I take a running jump anyway, knowing that if I land anywhere near, I can climb. I land right on the edge, and it's easy enough to stand up in front of the pyres, breathless and covered in blood and burns. I look straight behind me to double-check where the phoenixes were.

They're not far.

"Please save my daughter! Just take her!" the woman cries at me, pleading. "Please! Please!"

"No, mama!" the girl wails.

"I'm not leaving either of you," I tell them and give the mother a nod, understanding she doesn't care as long as I get her child out. I might not be a parent, but I know what she's asking me to do. I run to the girl and start undoing the ropes with my burnt hands. There are so many wraps of rope that it takes me longer than I hoped, and the flames of the phoenixes get closer and closer with every passing second. It's extremely hard to undo the rope, thanks to the cuffs, and I must push each layer of rope around her every time to untie it. I'm covered in sweat and blood and burns, but I push it all to the side to focus. I have to get her out. I couldn't live with myself.

The girl looks at me with pure panic in her eyes as her mum tries to soothe her, telling her repeatedly how much she loves her. It makes me think of my own mum and how she must feel about having me in this world, the world she fought to hide me from. The second the girl is out, I run to the mum and start undoing her.

"No, get my daughter away from here! They are coming!" she shouts at me, her voice pleading. "Please! Please!"

I look over at the phoenixes and know there is a slim chance.

"Help me pull the rope!" I tell the girl. She moves to my side, and we work together, pulling and untwisting the rope.

I can feel the heat of the phoenixes right before the rope falls, and she jumps out, grabbing her daughter. I look around us, seeing that the other side of this hill is a massive jump to freedom. We won't make it back over the crater, and the forest would hide us. It's a big jump, though, for a little girl. I look at the little girl, her little legs, and close my eyes.

"Dammit," I whisper to myself, thinking of anything to get us out of this. I have one idea that settles in my mind, something crazy, perhaps even insane. It probably won't work, but it might do, and it's the only way I see the girl surviving this.

I look down at the girl. "I want you to climb on my back and hold on tight. Can you do that?"

She looks at her mum, who nods at her and meets my gaze. "What's your plan, princess?"

"It's Riona, and you won't like it. I just need you to trust me and make that jump," I say, pointing at the gap.

Her eyes widen, and she looks between her daughter and me.

"Promise me you won't leave her?"

"I'd die first," I firmly state. "I'm not my father. I'll bring your daughter over, I promise."

She hugs her daughter tightly, whispering something to her and nodding at me. She runs and I hold my breath as she makes the jump over, slamming into the cliff wall. She grabs hold of rocks above her, and she starts climbing up the last bit as I hear squawking behind me.

I look towards the little girl, keeping an eye on the approaching phoenix. "What's your name?"

"Alyx," she tells me in a shaky voice.

"I'm going to do something completely and utterly insane, and I really need you to trust me and hold on. Ok?"

"Yes," she replies with nothing but fear in her tone. I have to do this. I can save her. I'm a goddamn queen, and I won't let the king of this hellhole force my hand.

The girl climbs on my back as I lean down, and holds onto me tightly like she's scared to even let go, and I don't blame her.

The phoenixes dive towards us, and they immediately start burning the first man, who never wakes up, and I really hope Alyx doesn't look, because I barely can. The smell is awful, and I'm glad the man doesn't wake. I can't save him. I keep my eye on the phoenix at the front, the biggest one and the best chance I have of doing this. It flies directly towards me, its red eyes and sharp beak so close as it snaps in my direction, and I slide to the side. I throw my arms around it and use the metal of the handcuffs like a collar to hold me to its body. It immediately lifts us off the ground and flies forward, trying to shake us off, and I lunge to the side. My stomach feels like it has a million butterflies in it as the phoenix swerves and shakes and tries to lean back to peck me, but the hold on its neck with my handcuffs makes it impossible. The girl screams, latching onto my back as I try to keep my eyes open, even as embers flicker into my face, down my hair, arms, and chest.

The scream stays lodged in my own throat as the handcuffs pull, pressured in the way they cut into my wrists. It almost feels like they could snap off. The phoenix flies directly in the way I want it to go, and I pull the handcuffs to make it turn right a little. It squawks and squeals at me as it fights, and I soon realise I haven't thought out the plan entirely, because when I let go, we're going to have a big problem.

It's going to be angry and ready to burn us to ashes.

The girl holds on tight, though, strangling me, and I hope she isn't getting burnt like I am. If she is, she doesn't cry out or say a word. As we come towards the edge of the trees, the second that I can, I let us go by sliding the handcuffs down its long body, and we both tumble to the ground. The fall hurts like a bitch, but I don't have a second to think about it. I grab Alyx's hand, pulling her to her feet as the phoenix spins around and lets out a long squawk, like the noise it made coming out of the ground.

Double fuck.

The phoenix flies up in the air and comes back down, squawking at us as we run into the trees where Alyx's mum is waiting.

"RUN!" I shout at them, and I run as fast as I can towards the tree line, the phoenix nipping at me from behind, catching my hair. Parts of it burn, but I try to ignore it, and I could barely feel the pain of the burns all over my body at this point. We head to the tree line, and it's easy to lose the phoenix as it backs away from the trees. I fall to my knees, the world getting dim and spinning.

Alyx kneels in front of me. "Are you okay? You look bad."

"Thank you is what my daughter meant," her mum says with a light laugh. "And do you need my help to stand? You need a healer."

"I doubt I'll be getting one in the prisons," I reply.

Alyx's eyes widen. "But you're the heir! Why would you be in the prisons?"

"My father," I reply. Her mum looks equally in shock and leans down, wrapping her arm around me to help me stand. The little girl goes to my other side and holds me up with her tiny arm. Every step hurts more than the last, the adrenaline wearing off, but we keep a good pace as we walk through the forest, back to Bane and Austin. Austin's eyes widen when he sees me, and he takes a step forward, looking devastated, but Bane puts his arm out to stop him.

I must look bad. Maddox is going to lose his shit.

Bane claps once as we stop in front of him. Alyx and her mum step back behind me, bowing their heads low.

"I said one. You've failed the test and now you must kill one of them. No spares," Bane demands.

"NO!" I scream at him. "I will not kill anyone, and neither will you! I've failed, sure you can say that, but killing either of them will make me hate you forever. It would be wrong, and you know that!"

"Fine," he replies.

One word, followed by one movement.

He spins and stabs a dagger through Austin's lower arm, cutting it off, and it falls to the floor before disappearing into flames. Austin's scream of pain is terrible, and it makes me scream too as I run to him, only for Bane to catch me, forcing me to watch as Austin screams and cries on the ground.

"LET ME GO!" I scream, fighting off Bane's arm.

"I told you one of them, and I'm being nice, daughter, but there is always a price. I hope his screams haunt you forever, because you caused this by not listening to me," he tells me calmly. I can't breathe, I can't think as I struggle to get to Austin, right before something slams into my head and darkness invites me, with a calm silence I will never get while I'm awake.

CHAPTER ELEVEN

The world is a mixture of pain as I drift awake and blink a few times to focus on Maddox as he holds me in his arms, my body in his lap. He isn't looking at me, but everything about him is tense, and the sting of the healed burns snaps me back into the reality of everything that just happened. The test, Alyx and her mum, and Austin. Gods, Austin.

"Austin..." I whisper, my voice cracking. Maddox looks down at me as I cry, feeling so powerless, so useless in every sense.

"I'm here, sweetheart," he murmurs in my ear. "And Austin is alive. I know that much. The healer who came to heal you told me and wanted you to know. Tell me everything when you're ready."

I nod, sobbing as I try to calm down. He might be alive, but it doesn't mean he is whole. I will never forget his screams, his cries of pain and what Bane did to his arm. There is no fixing that, hellcaster or not, and I hate Bane so much for it. Eventually I calm down enough to tell Maddox everything that happened in the test, and I swear he stops breathing when I talk about riding the phoenix with the handcuffs.

"And after Austin's arm was gone, Bane hit—" I pause as a sharp pain lances across my chest. I look down and pull my top to the side, seeing the white veins of the curse crawling across my chest.

I look up at Maddox, his jaw tight as he looks away. "I've only ever wanted to protect you, and I am failing. I am failing you."

"No, you're not," I softly say, cupping his cheek and turning his face to mine, his beautiful dark eyes locked on mine. "We can't stop everything that happens to us, and we can't fight everything together. But just knowing you're here when I wake up, loving me, caring for me, is everything.

Maddox, you give me the strength to fight every single day."

"Be my mate, Riona," he asks me. It's not the first time he has asked, but the answer will always be the same. This seems like more than a question, though. It's like he wants to become mates right now. He runs his fingers through my hair, sending goose bumps down my spine. "When they brought you in here, covered in burns and unconscious, I realised I don't want to wait anymore. I lost it, Riona, and barely let the healer treat you."

He pauses. "I love you, and I want us to be mates when we face your father next. I want us to be mates in case anything happens and mostly because I love you more than anything in this world or the next."

"Until the stars fade from the sky," I whisper back. "And even after, I will always love you. Through the darkness and through the never-ending night, I will be your light."

His eyes light up, and he leans down, kissing me softly. "I've seen a mating, most of it, and know the words. You will have to repeat them."

"Then what?" I ask.

He runs his fingers down my arms. "Then I bury myself inside you and claim you, Riona."

"But the guards?" I whisper, a thrill of pleasure shaking down my body.

"None in here," he tells me with a dark and wicked smile. "Are you ready?"

I brush some of my hair out of the way and look up at Maddox. "I was born to be yours, Maddox."

He leans down and captures my lips in a scorching kiss that curls my toes. He moves us so we are sitting cross-legged, facing each other on the bed. I glance at my oversized brown top and black leggings, wishing I was wearing something nicer.

Maddox is wearing a soft black shirt and ripped black trousers, and he looks amazing even if he wore nothing.

Maddox takes off his shirt, and I suck in a breath at the sight of his muscular chest. He always takes my breath away. He rips the shirt up into a long piece of fabric and takes our hands. Maddox ties our wrists together, carefully avoiding the handcuffs that are a weight on my soul.

Maddox pauses when our hands are tied and looks me dead in the eye. "Riona Dark, I take thee as my mate and offer up my soul."

I repeat his words. "Maddox Borealis, I take thee as my mate and offer up my soul."

His eyes are burning through me as a new tension builds in the room, and the air begins to feel like magic. It crackles in the air like electricity, but I hardly notice as I watch Maddox.

"*Anima mea ad te, Sanguis meus ad te; Anima mea ad tuum,*" he softly but firmly states, and I gasp, feeling something crashing into me. Into my soul. My eyes widen as I look behind us, and there is red energy in the air, flickering to life in swirls that flow from Maddox to me. It burns through the bindings around our hands and wrists, leaving more of the red energy in the air.

As I repeat the words, the red energy brightens and changes, getting thicker, and it almost covers us. Maddox is on me the second the last word leaves my lips, and I kiss him back with the same passion, a desperate need for us to mate. To take him as my own.

I rip at his trousers as he rips my top off and pulls my leggings off until we are both bare. His thumbs rub against my nipples as he kisses down my stomach. Maddox dives between my legs, a man on a mission, and his hot tongue swirls around my clit.

My back arches, and a moan escapes my lips that echoes around the room.

"You're mine," Maddox growls, kissing my clit one more time. "Mine."

His growl vibrates against me, and I cry out in pleasure as he slides two fingers into me at the same time he flickers and sucks my clit.

"Maddox, I—" I scream as I come hard, my orgasm shaking through my body as Maddox flips me over on the bed and slams into me. I moan as he thrusts, leaning over my body and brushing my hair to the side.

I arch my neck for him, feeling my second orgasm building, and the second he buries his teeth deep in my neck, as deep as his cock is inside me, I come again. He thrusts hard and fast as he drinks from me, and I can't feel anything but Maddox as he takes me as his mate, marks me as his, and I wouldn't have it any other way.

"Riona," he groans against my neck as he comes inside me. We collapse to the bed, and he pulls me into his arms, the room still buzzing with the red energy of our mating. As I focus on breathing, I feel the mating bond clicking into place and binding our souls as deep as anyone can be bonded. I can feel Maddox, like a sixth sense, and it's amazing.

"Why did we wait to do this?" I question with a slight laugh.

He darkly chuckles, holding me to him. "I'm not sure."

"Wait," I say, sitting up and looking down at my handcuffs. I'm not tired anymore, and something is different...my magic is leaking out of the barrier. I look up at Maddox, and he tilts his head to the side.

"My magic is going to you," I whisper. "We are sharing it."

"I can feel it," he murmurs and gives me a sinister smile before grabbing the cuffs. His hands immediately glow with red magic, the orbs' magic that we now share. The cuffs melt into red dust that falls onto the bed.

I take a deep breath of freedom.

"My queen, shall we kill the king?" Maddox asks, rising from the bed after pulling on his clothes. I get dressed quickly after cleaning up and look at the bars. I hold out my hand and slam my power into them, and they melt down into puddles on the ground. I look at the silver dress next, and the vision flashes into my memory as I burn it into nothing. I will not be the heartless, empty queen I saw.

"The only king here is you. It's about time this world bowed. Don't you think?"

Maddox's dark smile mimics my own. He might be the villain, but together, we are going to be Bane's worst nightmare.

This world is getting new royalty.

CHAPTER TWELVE

"Kneel before your queen and king or die," Maddox coldly demands to the guards who wait at the top of the stairs. There's five of them, and they all fall back, moving away from us. One of them I recognise because of the silver crest on his jacket. Three of them instantly pull out their swords and light them up with flames before running at us. Maddox barely even moves before he is on them. He rips the throat out of one of them before the guard even realises Maddox is there, and the others, he burns into nothing as he feeds off the guard in his arms. His eyes stay on me as he drains the hellcaster and lets him fall to the ground with a thump that echoes around us. As

Maddox walks to me, we both see the last two guards are kneeling with their heads bowed.

I look at the guard in the middle, and he raises his helmet. "Pass the word to your soldiers, to your guards, to anybody here in this castle. Leave. Leave and get out of here, because this castle isn't going to be standing for long."

He takes off his helmet, revealing greying black hair, an aged face and bright golden eyes. "Yes, my queen. My name is Gordian, and I am glad you broke out of the handcuffs. They were made with phoenix hearts, the strongest metal in the worlds."

"Good man," Maddox replies as he takes my hand, linking my fingers.

"Where are my mother and my brother?" I ask.

He points at the staircase on the right. "Go up. They're both heavily guarded, so it shouldn't be hard to find."

A few guards come running down the corridor, and Gordian holds his hand up. They instantly stop.

"Evacuate the castle, get your families, and run for the borders of the city. NOW!"

The guards don't need told more than once, and Gordian looks down at me.

"Don't kill the guards unless you have to. Yes, we have followed the king for a very long time, and it's all we've ever known. I was trained since I was a young child, and I don't remember my parents. All I remember is serving the king and learning to fight and being this. This is what everyone in this castle is like. Show us a bit of mercy and you will find a castle full of hellcasters who will worship you for a chance at freedom. None of us like being here," he tells me and bows his head. "Alyx is my daughter. You saved her and my mate. I owe you so much."

"Get them out of here," I tell him.

"Yes, my queen," he replies before running away.

We head down the corridor, which is thankfully empty, and come to two more staircases, and I hear the shuffle of feet on the staircase above on the right side where Gordian said to go. He could be leading us into a trap, but I don't think so. I saved his mate and child. Hopefully that is enough. We go up together and come to a corridor full of guards, seven on each side standing against the walls, and behind them are two doors. They instantly turn to us, and I nod at Maddox before we clasp our hands together. A wave of red energy slams out of us, blocking the hellfire that they threw our way. The orbs' magic slams into each of the guards and knocks them unconscious one by one until they're nothing but piles of bodies in armour on the floor.

"I can see why my father liked this power so much," Maddox says.

"I have to admit I quite like it myself," I reply. "Let's split up."

"I don't like the idea of leaving you, my mate," he replies.

"I know, but we need to find them, and we don't have much time before Bane gets here and we fight him," I remind Maddox.

"Okay, but call for me if you see Bane. Destroy anyone in your way," he commands.

I wink at him and go to the door on the right. Maddox goes into the left door, and I watch him before going through the right door. I'm surprised to see Katy as she slams her dagger through a guard's throat, and he convulses before falling on the floor at her feet.

"About time," she says, wiping her bloody dagger on her white maid dress. She rips the dress off, revealing her leather clothes underneath. "Don't feel bad for him. He touched my ass, so he deserved it."

I make sure to kick the bastard as I step over him to Katy, who is still talking. "Your mum's back there getting her stuff and changing her clothes. I was getting her out either way."

"Thank you," I say, wrapping her in a hug. She doesn't hug me back and stands stiffly for a long time, like she doesn't know how to hug.

"I don't do hugs," she reminds me.

"I know, but I do," I tell her, letting go, and she rolls her eyes at me, but I see a hint of a smile. "Please tell me we're getting out of this place. I need to see snow again. I cannot stand all this heat, and the hellcasters are pretty lame," she questions.

"I'm half hellcaster," I remind her.

"I said what I said," she replies, and I chuckle, walking towards my mum's bedroom. "Maddox is in the other room across the corridor. He might need help with Austin."

"On it," she says and runs out the door.

I feel nervous for some reason as I open the bedroom door. "One second, Katy. I can't leave without a cloak to protect me from hellfire—"

My mum pauses as she pulls on a red cloak as she turns to me, realising I'm not Katy. We both pause just for a second before we're running towards each other. I throw my arms around my mum and hold her tight like I've never hugged her before in my life, and I never want to let her go.

"My daughter, my daughter, my daughter," she says in an emotional rush, cupping my cheeks and leaning back. "I'm so sorry. I'm so, so sorry. I should have told you about all of this. This was never the plan. I was always going to keep you safe from him and explain this all. I—it just went all wrong."

"I know," I softly say. "But you kept me safe all those years. You gave me an amazing childhood and not one part of me hates you for it. Ok?"

"Really?" she asks, and I nod. She kisses my forehead and hugs me one more time.

"But we really do need to get out of here, because we are leaving this hellhole and going back to The Onyx. I have someone I want you to meet properly. Maddox, my mate."

"Your mate?" she asks softly. There's a bit of sadness in her eyes because her mate, he is what he is.

"Bane has to die," I tell her. I hate that I'm killing someone she is bonded to, because she will feel it, but he can't live. He can't escape this world, because so many would die, and no one would be able to stop him.

"What do you know about bonded mates, Riona?" she asks me, picking up a small bag and throwing it over her shoulder.

"Plenty, but this isn't the time. We have to get Austin and go."

"If he dies, so do I," she replies, and everything goes still. "But I want you to kill him. You're right. He can't live."

"No," I say, shaking my head, but it's true. I know this, Maddox told me, but I never thought about it when it came to my mum. I always knew I'd die in a heartbeat without Maddox. The only way to survive your mate dying is with a lot of magic. The orbs' magic is the only way known or surviving death is rare. The orbs' magic kept Maddox's father alive, but his mind was different, and he was cruel. It broke him. I can't let my mum be broken. I can't let her die either. "We'll find a way to break the bond and keep you alive. It's not happening. You're not dying, Mum."

"Riona—"

"No," I say, my voice cracking. I finally have my mum back, and I am not losing her. "No."

"Riona, come on!" Katy shouts, and I walk to the door, leaving that conversation in this room. I won't watch my mum die.

"Let's go," I tell my mum. Her eyes are ringing with sadness, but she follows me out into the corridor. Katy and Maddox have Austin between them, his arm a bloody stub wrapped badly, and he looks feverish.

I rush to him, my mum doing the same, and she cups his face. "He is burning up. My poor boy."

"I've given him some blood. It will keep him alive," Katy tells my mum. "But the arm is gone, and I think he has an infection in it. He needs a healer."

"The castle is evacuating. We have no chance of finding a healer," I say, hearing the noise behind us, the sound of so many hellcasters running out of here.

"We need to go," Maddox says and nods at the corridor. "Lead the way, sweetheart."

Mum stays close to Katy, and I lead the way, making sure my hands are full of my magic in case anyone comes this way. I get three steps in before I hear a screeching noise echoing around us. It's like an alarm, but it's not normal, echoing through the entire castle so loud it hurts my ears. "What the hell is that?" I ask.

Mum looks at me with a little confusion. "It's an alarm that goes off when there's been a portal opened and someone's coming. It went off last when you came to this world with Katy."

Katy smiles at me. "It's really about time his pretty ass turned up here."

"How do you know he has a pretty ass?" I ask with a grin.

She raises an eyebrow for an answer.

"I really, really hope you're not talking about my brother's ass," Maddox mutters in disgust.

"We are—" I say at the same time Katy says, "We are not," and I laugh a little with her.

"Come on," I say, turning down the corridor. The alarm never ends, making me wonder how big the portal is and how many of our people Reign is bringing through. We need an army to take Bane down, and I trust Reign to have that part handled. After going down a long winding staircase, we come out on a veranda that overlooks the front gates of the castle and a big space underneath it. The room is full of hellcasters running out of the door, carrying bags and anything they can as they escape. The word got out, it seems. I'm happy to see a bunch of the hellcasters who are running are

G. BAILEY

guards, and they look like they are getting their families out. They barely even look our way or notice us in their escape, and I look down, knowing he is there without finding him right away. Bane stands in the middle of the doors, still as a statue as his people run past him.

The look of betrayal on his face is completely and utterly priceless as he stares at us all.

"Katy, take my brother and mum and get them to Reign. Get them out of this castle," I instruct her.

"I'm not going anywhere," my mum firmly states. "I started all this, and I will help end it. Katy, take Austin and keep him safe."

"I can—can help...," Austin groans, trying to push off Maddox's grip. Maddox pats his head and says something quietly to him, and whatever he says seems to calm him. Maddox lets Austin go, and Katy helps him stand.

"Stay safe," he tells me. "I need my pain in the ass sist—sister."

"I love you, bro," I tell him. Mum speaks quietly to him as Maddox steps to my side, and we head to the top of the steps. A few stragglers are leaving the room as Mum joins us at the top of the stairs, and Bane walks to the bottom. I look over to see Katy leaving through the door on the other side of the corridor.

I trust her to get to Reign and to keep my brother safe. Katy is a good friend, a loyal vampire, and I owe her a hell of a lot for everything.

Bane pauses at the bottom of the steps. His gold shirt and dark trousers don't match the crown on top of his head, and I don't know why it stands out to me, but it does.

"You would really side with them over me? Your mate?" he asks her, his voice easily echoing through the small space between us.

"Oh, Bane," she says, holding her head high. "I once felt completely and utterly in love with you. I knew you were a monster. Part of me always knew. I saw the things you did, and I tried my hardest to push them from my mind. I hoped you'd change. When you told me you'd change for me, I believed it. You were kind to me, sweet and caring, so I believed you could be that way to the rest of the world."

She blows out a breath. "But it was a ticking time bomb, as you were pretending to be those things. You told me the only reason that you were lost in darkness was because you never found your mate, and I fell in love with that lie. We played happy family for a while, but all that time, you were lying to me. You were betraying me constantly. It was just a game to you because you don't have a clue how to love someone, let alone your own mate."

She looks over at me. "They're the only good things that ever came out of our mating, and part of me will always thank you for them. But no, I do not love you. I have not loved you in a long time. I loved a human who may not be my mate, but he was the kindest, gentlest man I've ever met. He brought up my children with me. No questions asked about who their real father was and why I was so scared of men. He was just there, and he was amazing. He was my best friend, and I will always love him."

It brings tears to my eyes to hear her talk about my dad like that, and I wish he was here. I wish he were alive.

I wish Bane hadn't killed him.

Mum looks over at Maddox. "You're different. I know you are. I foresaw you a long time before you met my daughter, and I always knew that between the pair of you, you would destroy this world, remake it and save these people. He's yours to kill, Prince Maddox."

She steps back and looks towards me and nods once.

Maddox flashes me a wickedly dark grin and picks up a sword someone dropped on the stairs. The sword lights up with the power of the orbs, glowing red.

"How is that possible?" Bane demands, his eyes flickering with darkness. "It's not possible!"

"When you have a true mate, you share everything. Including your souls and your magic," I say.

"My king," I whisper to Maddox and wink. "I believe this fight is yours."

Maddox steps away from me, prowling towards my father, who snaps.

"You will never be king!" Bane shouts at Maddox, who continues down the steps like a wave of darkness. Every footstep cracks the stairs with red magic, and I move to stand next to my mum.

"I'm so happy to see you find your equal. Love him forever, Riona," Mum whispers to me. "Always."

"Don't talk to me like you're going to die. You're not. I have a plan, and you are going to fight one last time for your children," I firmly tell her. "But first, let's watch a king finally die."

CHAPTER THIRTEEN

*I*t's hard to watch Maddox walk into this fight alone when I want to be there at his side, but something tells me that he needs to do this, and it shouldn't be me killing my father.

It should be him.

Bane has done a lot of things, killed a lot of people I love, and nearly destroyed me and my mate. He deserves this, and he always had this coming, from the second he decided to take my mum and brother and Maddox.

If he had treated his mate with kindness and looked after his people, maybe they would be in here defending him.

Instead, he is on his own, with his family watching his fall.

This is a fight between kings, and I will be here continuously supporting Maddox, because we both know that Bane does not have a queen supporting him.

He is alone.

And he will die that way.

Maddox walks to the bottom of the steps, and Bane starts to lose his appearance as a man and turns into something out of a horror film that I've seen once before. Bane is made of a pure red fire, and this other form is monstrous as he towers above Maddox at least eight feet. His arms are made of pure flames with sharp points like daggers at the ends, and on his back are spikes, along with a spiky tail. Every bit of him is on fire, and it flickers out.

He sort of resembles a man, but his face is long and protruding, like a wolf. Maddox isn't fazed as he lifts his sword and moves quicker than I can trace; he is on Bane. Bane must be able to track his movement better than I am, because he meets his sword with his arm, the clashing sound vibrating through the air. They both clash against each other again, and Bane uses his giant arms like swords to block and hit at Maddox.

The only difference is Maddox is faster, smarter, and he has the magic of the orbs. Maddox slams a sphere of magic into his chest, and it throws him back against the wall. The wall cracks and I watch the fractures slide up into the ceiling, knowing it's going to fall.

Bane roars, shaking the walls, and throws a wall of hellfire at Maddox. My heart lunges as I step forward, and Maddox stands still as the fire simply brushes through him.

He looks over, his dark hair lined with ash and his cheeks marked with dirt, and winks at me.

My mate can't be burnt, either.

"Take out the ceiling before it falls on Maddox," my mum suggests in a panicked voice. "Hurry!"

I build power in my hands, as much power as I possibly can into a giant orb. My mum stands back behind me to hide, and I can feel how scared she is. I quickly slam the magic up into the air through the castle ceiling where it spreads, destroying everything into red magic ash that falls around us. Red light pours in through the ash onto us, and I look down to see Maddox and Bane are locked in their deadly fight. Neither of them even notices what I've done as they hit each other again, and I'm not sure who is winning. My heart catches in my throat as Bane manages to get a hit on Maddox's arm, and Maddox hisses in pain before turning back and baring his teeth. That's when he sees a second sword on the floor, and he picks it up, swinging it around in his hand. This one lights up with the orb magic too as they both start circling each other once more. Maddox attacks first, crashing across the room.

I feel like I'm always connected to him, like I'm fighting there with him as one person, but I can only watch. I'm not a trained fighter, but Maddox is. He has been trained by his father and Reign since he was young.

He was trained to be a king that won the battles. Maddox springs off the ground, right over Bane's head, and swings to the side. It takes me a second to realise what he did as Bane howls in pain and his right arm drops to the floor.

Maddox did that on purpose, and he swings his bloody sword around in his hand. "An arm for an arm. Bastard."

Bane loses it, rushing at Maddox in a frenzy of hellfire, and he's almost animalistic in how quickly he moves. Maddox holds steady, waiting for him to get closer and casually moving out of the way. He spins as Bane turns and crashes into him, and he blocks him with his swords. They both crash against walls, knocking down everything in their path, and my soul feels out of control and will be until this battle is over.

Outside the castle, I can hear screams and shouting and more alarms going off and blasts, and god knows what is going on outside there. I try not to think about it. I try not to think about Katy and Austin out there getting to Reign. It's going to be nearly impossible for her to carry him all the way through the city. But if anyone can do it, it's Katy. Reign might have someone who can heal my brother, and it's better than being here right now with this fight. I watch as Maddox jumps into the air and slams his sword straight down into my father's chest, grabbing his neck at the same time, and he throws Bane across the room with the force of the hit. Bane collapses into the wall, choking as he starts to flicker back between forms. Maddox grabs his leg and drags him across the room before flipping him over his shoulders, slamming into the steps. Maddox is breathless as he stands over my father and roughly pulls the crown off his burning head. He holds the crown up in the air before letting it burn away into ash with the orbs' power.

"There'll be no king of the hellcasters. There'll be no king of this place. The Moral Fall City will be nothing but a memory, and you will be nothing at all," Maddox states. "My rule will outshine yours, and you will be forgotten."

He lifts his other sword, and my mum screams, even as Maddox slams his sword down and beheads the king. His head rolls down the bottom of the steps, and I look away, unable to watch, my stomach turning at the sight of all the blood. My mum suddenly stops screaming and goes still before collapsing to the floor. I fall with her and hold her in my arms.

"Maddox!" I scream, calling him over. He rushes up the steps, and he's at my side in a second. "Give her your blood. Turn her! Please!"

Maddox cuts his wrist and puts it over her mouth in seconds, feeding his blood to save her for me. He feeds her for a long time before she collapses asleep, and I lay her down on the floor.

Everything is so still for a while, and even as the city cries outside go silent, I hear nothing until I can feel my mum's heartbeat under my hand flare to life.

I suck in a breath and wipe the tears away from my cheeks. "Will she survive?"

"She'll be a d'vampire, but yes," Maddox says, standing up and wincing from the cut on his arm. I straighten up and go to his side, peeling back his shirt to have a look at the deep wound. "I will heal, sweetheart."

I shake my head, reminding myself that he heals quicker than I do. "We need to get outside and see what's going on. The city needs to know the king is dead and the war is over."

"I've got your mum," he says, leaning down to pick up my mum and throw her over his uninjured shoulder. I head down the ruined steps, dodging fallen pieces of the roof and tall piles of ash. I look down at what's left of Bane's body on the stairs. It's softly burning into embers before my eyes, and soon there will be nothing left. I make a decision to level this entire castle and this world once everyone is out.

He's nothing but dust, and no one should remember him. He should be nothing. I don't look back as we pass him and get outside onto the top steps. The steps go right down into the houses of the city on this side, and we are so high up we can see everything.

The city is at war. There are portals open everywhere, ripping apart the world, flooding it with incoming vampires and what looks like witches and sirens too. Hundreds of the houses and towers are burning and being blown up before my eyes. The streets are full of hellcasters, fighting or running from the portals and the vamps coming out of them. I catch a glimpse of siren magic, water flooding one street in the distance, and blasts of witch magic that light up areas in a way witch magic can do. Maddox gently puts my mum down on the steps in the corner where she's well hidden.

Everyone is being killed, and it's pointless. The hellcasters are fighting for a dead king and a war that they can't win with no leadership. I know not everyone in this city is evil, and the good should be saved.

"We need to stop this," I say, "before we all destroy each other. I don't want to be the queen of this kind of world. There has been enough war. We need peace."

"The orbs...the power. It could rip this world apart," Maddox suggests. "If we use it, it could mark a change. The hellcasters would stop. Everyone would."

I walk to Maddox and look back at my mum for a second. Maddox moves quickly down to the bottom of the steps and talks quietly with a bunch of hellcaster teenagers hiding before he whizzes back to me.

He pulls me into his arms and kisses me. He kisses me even as the world burns around us, and I love every second.

"I've been a villain for most of my life," Maddox whispers against my lips. "And you make me want to be a hero."

"You are," I whisper back. "Even lost in the darkness, you couldn't hide who you are."

"Save the world with me, sweetheart?"

"Okay," I reply and kiss him one more time in this mess of a world. "Let's burn it down."

CHAPTER FOURTEEN

REIGN

The hellcaster streets are in utter chaos, and it's a shithole of a city. No wonder they were trying to escape. Half the buildings look like they were ready to crumple before we even got here, and the army isn't any better. They don't have any control or direction, and half of the ones I've seen so far can just about throw a tiny ball of hellfire. I would be embarrassed if The Onyx army was in this state.

My trained vampires move as a unit across the streets, and I don't have to look their way to trust what they are doing. They are under strict instructions to only fight those who attack first and to find our missing royals, Katy, and Riona's family. There is a surprising number of women and children, who are told to stay in their houses as we head through the streets. Surprisingly, not a lot of hellcasters have attacked our army, and we were prepared for a much bigger fight.

"No sign or news of the queen and Katy," one of my vampires tells me, and I nod at him. I need to find Katy more than I want to breathe.

I need to find my brother and my sister-in-law, but I have a feeling they can look after themselves. I come to the top of a large hill filled with hell-casters running away from a giant castle at the other side of the city. It's falling to pieces even before my eyes, and there is a giant hole in the ceiling. I'm going to take a wild guess that's where my brother is. He's always in dead centre of some kind of massive destruction. I walk down the streets, watching as hellcasters run into their houses with wary glances at my vampires standing guard and mapping the city. The sirens send water splashing over the towers on fire, trying to save whoever is inside. The witches caused the fires, and I'm not sure it was an accident. I fought for the alliance between the sirens' new queen, Natalia, and me. She wasn't queen until a week ago, as apparently she decided to fight for Riona and the future she offers.. The previous queen, Andraste, was still pissed that we took Riona and was happy to not help us at all. Natalia is a friend, she came to me, and I see a long alliance between us all.

There's no need for us all to be at war when there is a magical orb-bearing queen in the world. She gives us life. Power. Safety. We can rather all share the power and share everything that comes with it, including the ability to have children, or we all end up alone, cold, and empty. Well, at least they would, as Riona would be ours either way. Whereas the alliance with Natalia came easily, Sabina was another matter. She might be Riona's aunt, but she is a cold woman with only her own goals that she cares about. After careful talks with her daughter, they decided it was a good idea to side with us. I'm still going to watch them, though, carefully. I don't trust Sabina at all, especially on her quest for power. She would quite easily rule the world if she could.

But I don't think she's brave enough to go against Riona, and hopefully Riona's mother is alive and well. That might soothe the alliance a little better.

I am heading slowly down, further into the city, when I hear a massive commotion. I rush ahead and I'm surprised. Well, I'm not completely surprised, because Katy is always in trouble, but there she is with five guards surrounding her, and she's fighting them off on her own, protecting a body behind her.

Every single time I see Katy, she takes my breath away with how fucking beautiful she is. Her black hair is in a braid down her back, her eyes sharp and stunning as she assesses the area. She moves as fast as lighting, her curvy body made to entice me.

And only me.

Using my vampire speed, I'm at her side in seconds, but I pull my swords out with a grin. My vampires stay back, knowing this is personal.

No one, and I mean no one, threatens my woman and gets away with it.

They die.

Now.

I fight the untrained hellcasters, knocking them down like dolls. Idiots. I knock three of them down in a blink, beheading two of them. I turn to see Katy pulling her sword out of one of the hell-casters, and I throw my sword into the neck of the last one, who is running away. It hits perfectly, and he falls.

I smile as she throws herself in my arms and kisses me like we have been apart years. Fuck, it felt like it. I didn't see Katy at my side for years. I knew she was there, but I didn't see her. Really see her.

It's that classic saying, you don't know what you have right under your nose. I had the whole fucking world, and I am never letting her go. I kiss her back, dropping my sword and sinking my hands into her soft hair, tugging her body against mine.

"I missed you," I tell her.

"I don't do sappy shit," she replies, making me laugh before capturing her lips one more time, loving how she leans into me, bending to my will and letting me take control.

A building nearby blasts apart, sprinkling embers and rocks down on us, and only then do I let her go, enjoying the dazed look in her eyes and her pink cheeks.

A groan makes us both look down, and I realise it's Austin, Riona's brother, and he isn't in good shape.

"Have you given him blood?" I ask Katy, leaning down over Austin and taking in his lack of arm and ear, and how pale he is.

"Yes, but he needs a witch healer," Katy says. "Riona sent me with him. Maddox was fighting Bane."

I nod and stand. "Get him through one of the portals to The Onyx. There are witch healers waiting to help anyone who comes through."

"Witches helping?" Katy says, picking up Austin over her shoulder.

"Escort—" I stop mid-sentence when I see why everyone has gone silent. Every single person in this world seems to have paused, looking up above the castle. Maddox and Riona are floating up in the air, smothered in red orb magic that I remember from my father. He used to use the magic like that but in a deep, horrible red colour. Their colour is different. It's bright, and it's glowing, almost a rainbow of colours underneath them, and they're floating in the air right above

THE IMMORTAL AND DAMNED

the castle, drawing in everyone to see them. They look like a star almost, but I feel completely awestruck by the power spreading from them. It's like a cobweb, spreading through the air and out of their feet into the ground.

They're sharing the power.

I didn't even know that was possible. We really have a new king and queen. I never thought my brother would be king, and I was literally named to be the king. But right in this moment, it feels perfect, like it was the right thing all this time. He was born to be king, and I was born to be at his side, his advisor.

His brother.

I watch as they rise in the air, almost swirling around each other, holding hands, and I realize they're building energy like a ticking time bomb.

What the hell are they doing?

"I need to get to them," I tell Katy. "And you need to get back to our world safely."

"Not without you," Katy demands. "They are dangerous!"

"Not to me," I reply. "They are my family, and whatever they are doing, I need to be there."

I whistle and four of my guards are at my side instantly. "You take Princess Katy back to our world and help her get Austin straight to a healer."

"Yes, sir," one of them answers and carefully takes Austin off her, carrying him easily with another one of the guards. The other two move to Katy's side.

"Princess?" Katy asks in disbelief, like she just realised being with me meant she would be part of the royal family.

"Yes," I firmly state with a smirk. "The second we get back, I'm literally going to tie you to my bed for weeks, and you're not leaving unless you're my mate."

She leans up and kisses my earlobe. "Who says I'll be the one tied up?"

This woman.

I growl at her, and she growls back before stepping back. The guards heard, and there are a few awkward coughs.

"Didn't know vampires got coughs, or are you all choking?" Katy asks.

Wisely, none of them answer as I chuckle. Forever with the most sarcastic, sexy-as-fuck Katy is a life I want.

I kiss her cheek before running straight towards the castle. I want this damn war to be over, and I want her in my bed permanently. I try to push my thoughts from Katy to focus on the task at hand. Maddox and Riona's power that they're building seems to rise, getting stronger and brighter, cracking the paths and towers, sending hellcasters screaming as they run out. It's almost hard to run towards them, the light and magic pushing me away. The city is a maze, and there's so many people around, it's hard to jump in between them as they go in the opposite direction to me. Eventually, I decide to climb one of the houses and start jumping over the rooftops, ignoring the sting of the orb magic above me.

Finally I get to the bottom of the castle steps, and I run to the top of them, right where Maddox and Riona are floating above me. I pause, surprised to see an older blonde woman tucked in the stairs, completely out of it. I don't know why, but she looks extremely familiar.

Someone is right behind me, and I instantly flip around and grab the boy's throat. I let go when I realise that he is a young teenager, and he coughs, stepping away with his hands up.

"The glowing man said to look for you. To tell anyone that's a vampire that this woman is Queen Riona's mother and should be cared for," the boy says before running away from me down the steps. I look at Riona's mother, struggling to remember her name and wondering what is wrong with her. I can't see any injuries or reason for her to be out of it, but I do scent Maddox's blood.

Could she be changing?

I pick Riona's mother up in my arms, noticing how she looks like Riona but a little older. Part of me can't wait to have her wake up, because she knew my father, and I believe we met once.

And she can sort her damn psychotic sister out.

I look up at the glaring light and make the decision to get Riona's mother out of here. Maddox has this under control. I hope.

I run down the steps, coming to a halt when I see Sabina at the bottom of the steps. Her eyes fixate on her sister, and to my surprise, she falls to her knees. The emotion on her face looks wrong, like a statue that's finally learnt how to smile. I really, really don't like it.

"I never, ever thought I'd see her again," she says, and I watch her cautiously.

"We should get out of here. It isn't safe," I say as Sabina rises and walks to me.

"I sensed her in the city and came for her. I don't know what your queen and king are doing, but we are leaving. Give me my sister."

"How can I trust you to not hurt her?" I question.

"I would never. She is blood," Sabina harshly replies. "And she is sick. Changing into a d'vampire. She needs a healer to guide her body and soul from witch to d'vampire safely."

I know she is right, but I also know she treated Riona like dirt. I don't have time for this. "Hurt her, and it will be Riona who comes for you."

Sabina pales at that and clicks her fingers. Riona's mum floats out of my arms and follows behind

Sabina as she walks away, several witches appearing out of the shadows and picking up Riona's mother. They are running in the next second, with a shield of darkness around them.

A long ringing noise echoes in the air, and I look up just as Maddox and Riona's power seems to explode.

It takes out the city in a hail of red magic, and the wave of magic heads right to me.

I can't escape it or outrun it, so I do the best I can and stand proud, thinking of only one person in these last few seconds.

I wish I had forever with her. My Katy. The woman I am completely in love with.

The red magic slams into me, and the next second, I feel like I can't breathe under piles of red ash. I close my mouth and push some of it away as I climb out and gasp in the fresh, salty, and cold air.

Pure sunlight shines down on me, and the soft sound of waves fills my ears as I take a minute to realise what they did.

They destroyed the hellcaster world and took all of us out of it unharmed. Thousands of hellcasters fill the beach, the sea and forest in the distance, buried in the red ash that has carried over. I wipe some of the ash from my eyes, looking for anyone I recognise.

I see them first, on a deck, and they are kissing, oblivious to us all.

"Bow to your queen and king. All hail our saviours."

Like a wave, the hellcasters, vampires, sirens, and witches on the beach fall to one knee as I do. They cheer Maddox and Riona's names, and I look up at the stars above.

Long live the rightful king and queen of The Onyx.

CHAPTER FIFTEEN

I missed my home.

Looking over the salty, sand-filled shores of The Onyx brings me back to the first time I stepped onto this strange and unique land.

I was terrified, alone and fearing for the future, but little did I know it was all leading me to my mate, to my crown and the future I was meant to have. I never would have believed this place could be my home, but it is, and it's the only place in the world I want to live with my family. I finally step off the ship, onto the decking. I feel different and free.

I'm finally free and home.

It's been three months since we broke the hell-caster world down into nothing and brought the hellcasters to our island, offering them peace and a world where they could be what they wanted and live wherever they like. A few thousand of them decided to go live in the human world under the promise that if they caused any trouble or killed anyone, then I'd be sending vampires after them to bring them back to face the consequences. We have vamps keeping an eye on them, and so far, only a few have been brought back and locked up for life. Even if they don't live on The Onyx island or with the witches or sirens who also opened their doors, I'm still their queen, and Maddox is still their king. I don't know who they're more frightened of, but it's certainly one of us or both of us.

Maddox steps off after me, jumping into the sand, and links his fingers with mine. We spent the last month with the witches, doing what should have been done a long time ago and breaking the curse. It took a lot of animal sacrifices, some pretty strange magic and a hell of a lot of pain on my side. But finally, my hands are free of that god awful curse, and our lives are ours, ours to live forever because we're immortal.

I used to think all the vampires were immortal and damned, but now I realise they were never damned. This is one hell of a life.

I look up at Maddox, and he smirks at me, leaning down and kissing my cheek. "It's good to be home with you."

"Did you not like the witches' company these last few weeks?" I question, teasing him. I know he didn't.

"I really, really don't like all the black shit on that island and the awful food," he replies, his voice a dark purr. "And the eyes always watching us. I didn't have you naked nearly as often as I wanted."

"You literally wear black all of the time," I reply, ignoring the shiver of pleasure that goes down my spine from his flirting.

Sex with your mate is incredible, and if I thought I couldn't get enough of Maddox before we were mates, it's nothing on now. I want him all the time.

"Yes, but red is definitely more my favourite colour," he whispers to me. "Like the panties and bra you have on that I'm going to rip off with my teeth."

He captures my lips in a deep kiss before I can reply, and I almost moan, my knees weak from one single brush of his lips.

"Brother!" Reign shouts in the distance, and Maddox takes his time kissing me before letting go, his eyes flashing with a promise.

This will be continued.

Maddox steps to my side as Reign and Katy run, stopping a few feet away.

"Why are you two always kissing on this beach with an audience?" Katy asks as a way of saying hello.

Maddox laughs and gives his brother a manly hug as I walk to Katy. I hug her tightly and she pats my back.

It's an improvement.

"Why do you smell different?" I ask randomly and out loud, when I didn't mean to.

Maddox chuckles, wrapping his arm around my waist and pulling me to his side. "She's pregnant. Congratulations, both of you."

"That's amazing!" I say cheerily. Katy sighs and steps to Reign's side, resting her head on his arm. They literally mated days after we came back from the hellcaster world, and they didn't leave their bedroom for weeks, so I'm not that surprised to hear she's pregnant.

I love kids, but for a long time, I'm taking a witch solution to stop pregnancies. I want to spend a good fifty years with my mate and sort out the mess of The Onyx so that humans do not have to fear living here and there is some kind of peace.

Peace takes time. I'm happy to be auntie, and I will adore their child.

"It was a surprise, but not an unwelcome one," Katy says. "I don't know how to look after a baby, but there are plenty of babies on the island now from the hellcasters, and I can learn."

"Can we go back up to the castle and say hello to everybody?" I ask Maddox, and he nods.

"Good to see you, brother. I expect to see you at dinner tonight," Maddox says.

"We will be there," he replies. "And I have a lot to update you on, King Maddox."

"Brother," Maddox replies with a smile. I love the relationship they are building now and how happy they both seem. Reign is relaxed and happy with Katy and his title as royal advisor to the king. I don't think Reign ever really wanted to be king.

Maddox was born for this. He is a good king because people naturally follow him, and he can make good decisions when he wants to.

He is still a bit of a villain, but what king isn't?

Maddox picks me up and, using his vampire speed, runs us off the beach and through to where the royal carriage is waiting with a driver. Maddox helps me into the carriage and pats the side before closing the door. The carriage takes off, and Maddox immediately starts pushing up my knee-length dress and pushing me back onto the seat.

"Maddox," I whisper as he exposes me to him, covered only with the red panties he talked about earlier.

The carriage bounces on something, and Maddox looks up at me. "Hold on, my queen."

I moan as he grabs my ass and rips off my panties, tearing them with his teeth. He dives between my legs, pulling my ass to the edge of the seat and licking all the way up my slit to my clit. I moan and arch my back, digging my hands into the seats. He growls against my core and flicks his tongue faster against my clit, his hands digging into my ass.

I come hard and fast, moaning so loud I place my hand against my mouth to stop the noise from escaping. Maddox picks me up and sits on the seat, placing me on his lap. He undoes his trousers and pulls out his hard, long and thick cock.

If his cock could win medals, it would get gold.

"Keep looking at him like that and I will never stop fucking you," Maddox whispers into my ear, pulling me close and lining me up. He runs the tip of his cock up and down my sensitive clit, and I moan.

He finally loses control and aims his cock, and I sink down on him. His eyes close in pure pleasure, and I love seeing him like this.

I rock my hips, building up speed, and he guides me for a moment before focusing on pulling my dress off. He cups my breasts through my bra, constantly fucking me as he rips it off.

He stares at my breasts like they are pure gold. I ride him slowly, enjoying him looking at me like this.

"My queen, you're fucking killing me with how sexy you are."

His dirty words just turn me on more. I moan, getting close to another release, and he leans forward, licking my hard nipple. I moan and ride him harder, his cock hitting a spot inside me perfectly with every single movement.

I rock my hips and he groans, kissing his way up my chest and to my neck. Right as I'm about to come, he bites into my neck at the spot he loves, and I cry out in ecstasy as I come. He repeats my name against my neck as he finishes inside me, adding to the pleasure I'm feeling as he hits deep.

I rock on him for a second as I calm down, and he releases his teeth.

"I will never tire of this," Maddox says, still inside me. "You have half an hour to say hello to everyone, and then I'm fucking you in my bed. For hours."

I shiver at his command.

Yes. Hell, yes.

I barely get my clothes back on as we get to the castle, and I still end up with no underwear, but Maddox gives me his cloak to tie on, and it hides my body, anyway. My cheeks are extremely bright red as the carriage comes to a stop.

"What is it with you in carriages?" I ask.

He laughs. "It's just *what is it with you?* I want you constantly, Riona."

"Good, because you have me forever, Maddox."

"I love you," he replies before he opens the door and helps me out. This cold castle used to be something I feared once a long time ago. Now the red snow, the towers built into the mountains as it looks over our city, is our home completely. It's filled with all the people I love. Standing at the door is my mum next to Austin, who looks a million times better than when I last saw him, and Arlo is holding his hand.

It's been a hard few weeks for Arlo after his little girl was born early, but with the witches help, she will live and thrive. He sent me a few texts, and I'm happy to be back here, to just support him the best I can.

Austin looks sad, which I think is more than just seeing Arlo have a baby with someone else. It's the loss of his arm. We discussed with the sirens and witches, and it can't grow back or be replaced by magic. There was no way of healing it back to what it used to be, and it's a permanent reminder of what our father did to him.

He broke something in Austin in those weeks down there. I know it did. My brother is quieter, more reserved than he's ever been, but I have high hopes that Arlo will heal something inside of him.

And the little girl who follows Austin around, making him occasionally smile. Ember. In my letters, Austin and Arlo explained Ember took the room near theirs, and they love her company in the cold castle. I really like that. She's definitely become my ward, but I have a suspicion they will be her dads.

I walk up, and I hug Mum first, her powerful arms tightening around me. It was touch and go with her too, and if it weren't for my Aunt Sabina, I don't know if Mum would have made it through the change. We didn't know whether it was going to work as she didn't wake up for over a week, but she fought her way back. I'm so glad she did. Sabina has been coming here often to see my mum and to make amends. I don't think I can ever fully trust her, but as long as she never brings Cross here, I won't say anything because my mum asked me to trust her on Sabrina. Plus, Sabrina wouldn't stand a chance if either Maddox or I decided to kill her, and she knows it.

"How was the trip?" Mum asks, like we were on vacation. I chuckle. We wanted her to come, but the witches aren't all in agreement, and it brought up issues with Sabina that we didn't want to affect breaking the curse. "It was okay, but the curse is gone. That's all that matters."

"We heard that, but I'd like to see," she demands in her mum's voice. I lift my arm out of the cloak, and everyone looks happy to see nothing but pale skin.

"It worked and I'm finally free," I say. "Not a curse in sight. Thank you for finding her, Arlo."

"Anything for family," he replies. Arlo never once rested in his search for the witch, and no one could have found her as quickly as he did. Luckily, she'd already had four children and lived in a nice little cul-de-sac in America, and she was more than happy to help once she believed Arlo about the witch's curse. The curse is broken, and no one will ever pay that price again. I look at Maddox and smile.

"It's over. It's completely and utterly over," I whisper, more to myself, but I know he hears me.

"Now we just have forever," Maddox replies.

"Did you hear about Reign and Katy? They're having a baby!" Mum says. I love how she is so close to Reign and Katy, and she treats us all like her children. Even Maddox. "Isn't it brilliant?"

"It is," I reply with a smile before going to Austin.

"Welcome back, sister," he says, letting me hug him. Arlo hugs me next before shaking hands with Maddox.

"Ember has been doing drawings for you both," Arlo says. "And all of them are on your bedroom wall because she's taken a real liking to that hawk, who seems to love her."

"I don't know if a giant hawk and a small child are a good mix," I say with a chill.

"She is literally a fire-breathing child. I'd be more worried for the hawk," Austin replies, and I laugh.

We all head to the castle to get out of the cold, and I'm surprised to see Hector in the entrance hall. I come to a stop and look at Maddox, who doesn't look happy to see him.

"What are you doing back?" Maddox asks, none too friendly.

"I was happy to come back now that everyone's at peace and there's no war. See, I don't like war, and you can call me a coward if you like, because I am one, but I'm here and I'll cook for you forever if you wish," he replies and bows his head. "If you will take me."

"Did you know about Cross?"

"That he was a slimy bastard? Yes," he replies. "But I didn't know he was a witch and plotting against you."

I look to Maddox, and he nods once, just for peace. "Step one foot out of line and it will be your head. Got it?"

"Yes." He bows. "I will start on your dinner."

"Prepare a big meal," Maddox warns with a growl, and Hector is gone. I link my hand with Maddox, and we go into the main sitting room where everyone seems to gather. The fire is lit, and it's so cozy, just like I remember. I look forward to many nights curled up on the sofa with Maddox. Ember is sitting on the sofa, drawing on a sketch pad, and she drops it when she sees me. Ember runs over and flings her arms around me tightly. I hug her back and pop a kiss on the top of her head.

"You're looking amazing," she says. "No more of the curse stuff. It faded your light."

"It had. I've heard you've been drawing loads," I say.

"Yup," she replies. "I like drawing the day you finally can be crowned king and queen."

"I think it's about time for that," Mum says, sitting on the sofa. Austin and Arlo sit on the other one, and Maddox wraps his arms around me from behind as we stand.

"Definitely time. We were thinking perhaps a massive celebration all across the city, and the day could be celebrated every year," I say.

Everyone is busy on the island with the new homes that are being built, the changes with so many vampires getting pregnant, and schools being set up for the hellcaster children. There hasn't really been time to celebrate.

"We can bring in human food and lots of wine," Arlo suggests.

"As long as I get to keep the queen at the end," Maddox agrees with a possessive note. Everyone laughs as Ember brings over her sketchbook and shows it to us. It's a picture of all of us together, and I definitely have a very strange crown on top of my head with a big red ruby in the middle.

"Red's your colour," Ember explains, and her cheeks are red.

Maddox reaches over me and picks up the drawing. "Kid, this is brilliant. Can I keep it?"

"Yes!" she says cheerily.

"I've been looking after the greenhouse," Mum tells me, and I'm relieved that she did. Ann is in the castle, but it's a lot for her to do on her own. "It's such a beautiful room, and I'm thinking of extending it all down the side of the castle so Ann, you and I can really make something special to be used by all the castle staff."

"That would be amazing," I say, agreeing. "Thank you, Mum."

"Don't thank me. This castle is a dream, and I'm not leaving," she replies, her tone dropping. "I wish your dad could have seen it."

"He is with us," I softly say, placing my hand over my heart. "Always."

"Always," she agrees. "Maybe we could get a stone placed in the greenhouse with his name on it to honour him."

"I will get it made as soon as possible," Maddox says.

I smile at Maddox over my shoulder. "We are going to get changed, as we have been on the ship for a week."

"That's not what you smell like," Arlo jokes, and I flash him my middle finger when Ember is walking back to them and can't see.

He grins as Maddox leads me out of the room and to the door to the corridor. I look back once at my family and smile. This is everything we fought for, and it is worth all the pain.

We head down the corridor, which has some new lights fitted, and I think we are going to the bedroom, but Maddox stops me, and he tugs me down the corridor towards the dining room.

"Where are we going?" I ask him.

"I want to show you something," he replies in a secretive tone. We head through the dining room straight to the massive, lit, stone fireplace. I pause as he turns the head of the dragon on the one side and twists it all the way around, and there is a clicking noise.

"No way, is this a moving fireplace?" I excitedly ask.

He laughs at my excitement as the fireplace literally slides to the side, revealing a dusty corridor and staircase at the end.

"I wanted to show you this for a while. It's a royal secret," he explains, unhooking an oil lantern off the wall. "Our father showed me and Reign when we were young kids, but it's been a while since we used this room."

"What's in here?" I ask, really curious now. Old castles. Moving fireplaces and royal secrets. Sign me the heck up.

Maddox smirks at me before he lights the lantern with the flame from the fireplace and walks in, offering me his hand. I take his hand, and he guides me into the corridor, the thick stone walls freezing cold to the touch as I brush my fingers against them on the way down the staircase. The room smells untouched and old, but it's not damp, and there's no obvious noise as we head inside. Maddox tells me to wait by the staircase and works on lighting all the hanging lanterns around the room, slowly revealing it. It's beautiful. There were several old red and black gowns at the one side, hanging on the wall, and in the centre is a massive chest filled with gold coins and necklaces and other things. There are dozens of chests around the edges of the walls, and a few of the walls have solid gold ornaments and vases that look delicate but expensive.

At the back of the room, on a tall shelf, are four crowns, and two of them are tiny, maybe for children, made with twisted silver and little red jewels. In the middle, there are two large crowns. One is very clearly for a king, with jutting gold spikes all the way around and rubies attached to it. The other one is more delicate, smaller and a tiara in shape, with a large red ruby in the middle and small diamonds at the side, holding it up before being encased in silver and gold.

"This is the Royal Treasury," he explains. "All the boxes that line the room are filled with ancient gold. This room is filled with enough gold for us to protect our people for lifetimes."

"Why have you never used it?"

"My father didn't want human interference on the island and believed humans were just food,"

Maddox says, picking up a gold coin and flicking it in the air before perfectly catching it. "So, he wouldn't use it."

"We should," I suggest.

"I was thinking we could trade for human things to bring onto the island to modernise. More cars would be a good start. We need to catch up with the modern world," Maddox says. "And I never used this room before because I didn't see a future. Now all I see is the future with you."

My heart warms.

"I love the idea of modernising the island," I say with a big smile. "I really love that."

With the whole *no slavery* law we made instantly and with no human slaves on the island to do everything for them, the vampires aren't happy. Maybe if we gave them more human and modern things, like a TV for instance, they might not try to ignore our rules.

Or Maddox will kill them.

I'd take the TV option if I were them. Blood banks have certainly been a thing to get used to for the entire island, but not Maddox, who loves to feed off me, and being mates, my body never weakens. I can't say the constant orgasms are a bad thing. When we first came back and announced that there would be no more human slaves and that every human on the island was considered free and their own person, it did not go well. There were a lot of murders and a lot of issues. But after Maddox had to carefully sort out a few of them, it became clear that unless these rules were followed, you'd leave the island one way or the other.

The other way happened a lot when Maddox lost his temper. But then we set up and encouraged the use of blood banks. Humans go and donate once a month, and we plan to import blood from the outside world eventually, which will be easier now that we can pay. The idea of blood banks is so the humans can freely give blood if they wish to, and most do. We also let numerous humans go back to the human world, to their homes they were stolen from, but they had their memories wiped by witches before they left, so they didn't risk our safety. After a few weeks, we also set up a system of humans being paid to be blood donors, so the humans living here didn't have to suffer without work. Overall, it seems to work. We left

Reign and Katy in charge, so we'll have to ask them about how it's been the last few weeks. But we've been sending regular texts, and we've not had any issues.

So far, I think we aren't failing at being their king and queen, and we will keep working hard and keep fixing all the broken parts until it works. Maddox walks over and picks up the small tiara and comes right back to me. He places it on my head and runs his fingers down my cheek.

"It suits you," he murmurs. "I'm not surprised. Red is definitely your colour."

He picks me up in his arms, and I hug him tightly, kissing him softly, which soon ends with him carrying me to our room. I never wanted to be a queen, but from the moment I met Maddox, I wanted to be his.

I will always be his queen.

EPILOGUE

*T*he red snow of my home floats around me in a light breeze, and I reach out, catching one of the delicate snowflakes in the palm of my hand.

"Riona Borealis, daughter of my line," she says, her hair the same colour as the snow, and I lower my hand as she walks to me through the snowstorm that blocks out the rest of the world. My grandmother is glowing, quite literally, and she is wearing a similar dress as before. I didn't think I'd see her in my dreams ever again, even though she promised there would be three visits. It's been ten years since I saw her last and, on some days, I wondered if she was even real or just a dream I'd made up to protect myself and give myself hope in the hellcaster world.

I look around at all the snow that fills the mountain of my castle home I share with my family. Well, most of them. Reign and Katy moved into the castle five years ago when their third baby arrived, and it was easier for Reign to help Maddox and me, and still be close to Katy. Arlo and Austin have stayed living with us, and Arlo's daughter now lives with us too after her mum had five more children and she wanted some space and to be with her dad. The castle is full of children, happiness, and joy...a far cry from what it once was. My mum lives half the time at the castle and the other in a house she owns in the city, which doubles as a women's protection unit where any woman or child in the city can go to find safety. The Onyx has changed so much in the last ten years, and now we have roads, cars (not a lot of them as importing fuel sucks) and modern plumbing throughout the city, along with electricity. With the fortune Maddox had, we made deals with a few governments who already knew about our existence and were happy to keep us a secret.

It hasn't been an easy ride with freeing all the humans, but the anti-murder law has held, and we currently have a prison with fifty-two vampires and three hellcasters inside, living a hundred-year sentence with correction therapy.

Maddox just wanted to end them all, but I somehow talked him down off that cliff. As for being queen of hundreds of thousands of people...it's been something to get used to. The bowing, the gifts, the title, and crown.

Maddox makes it all worth it. As does The Onyx. It was once a cold, horrible island with just as horrible vampires living on it, treating humans as slaves. It's different now, and the last thing I would call The Onyx is cold.

It's bursting with life, literally, with all the kids around, and people are trying to learn about humanity.

"Do you know why the mountain always snows red?" I ponder, more to myself, but I say it anyway.

She laughs. "I'm dead and, instead of asking what it is like to die, you ask about snow?"

"I don't want to know what it's like to die," I reply with a small smile.

"There is a spell on the island that only red snow shall fall. Some witch cast it on her deathbed many, many years ago," she tells me. "But I am here to speak one more time to you, and we do not have long before your mate will wake you."

"You're here to say goodbye," I say, a part of me feeling sad. I don't know her well, but she is family, and she helped me.

"I am," she replies and steps forward. "But your child will be born in a few years, with hair like mine and eyes of red flames like your mate. I know a part of me lives on."

My child? Maddox will be happy to know there will be an heir around soon. Our own child. I've thought about it a lot over the last year, mostly with all the kids and babies in the castle. It's hard not to. Currently, Reign's oldest daughter is our heir, but Maddox wants a bunch of kids. I'm hoping he will be happy with one.

Maybe two.

"Boy or girl?" I ask.

She smiles. "You will find out soon, Riona. I am proud of you, so you know. Your dad is too."

My heart hurts as I give her a sad smile. "Tell him I love him so much."

"He knows," she softly replies. "And he is with you, as am I until the end."

"Thank you. I can't thank you enough for giving me the orbs; I could never have survived without them. And thank you for sacrificing your life to get them away from Bane. I don't know where any of us would be if you hadn't."

"Thank you for making me proud. Go and enjoy your life, Riona."

"I will," I whisper back, and I mean it. Every moment I have in my life feels special because I know what it is like to lose everything and everyone you love. This is a second chance, and I will never waste it.

"By the way, don't you have a secret to tell?"

I wake up slowly, the dream like a movie in my mind I can repeat over and over. Warm, toasty sunlight beams down on me, covering nearly all of my body as I breathe in the salty, warm sea air of Greece in the middle of summer. I rest my arm over my forehead to block out some of the light as I sit up and stretch and look around for him. My king. My lover. My mate. I find him instantly, his soul calling to mine in a way only mates can do. I could find him anywhere on earth, and he could find me, too. Maddox is in the water right in front of me, facing the ocean and watching the yacht floating in the sea, attached to the nearby dock.

Droplets of sea water, the emerald green and sea blue droplets, fall from his wet hair. His hair is long enough that it now hits his neck and shoulders, in locks of dark brown. I'm glad he's decided to grow it out again after cutting it, as I love running my fingers through it. The red crystals woven into his hair shine in the sunlight and catch my eye. There are three blue ones woven in, and Reign wears the other three. They both might have bad memories of their parents, but they did bring them up, and they chose to honour them in that small way.

The beautiful sunlight of our private beach in Greece shines down on us as I watch my mate in the sea. It's one of his favourite places in the world, and it's definitely in my top three. Maddox bought a villa and the private beach that goes with it five years ago for me as an anniversary present. We come here at the same time every year, and it's our way of getting away from the responsibilities of our life. We spend most of the year looking after the monarchy and being the king and queen they need. We spend a week or two sometimes being normal pretend-humans and mixing with the crowd. I spend most of the days on the beach, and we spend our nights in the cities, dancing and enjoying everything the world has to offer. The Greek people are the kindest in the world, or at least I think so.

Maddox is relaxed here...in a way I love to see. On The Onyx, there is always the pressure of so many people needing us, and here there isn't. We get to be free, for a moment, and it's something we treasure. Maddox looks back, spotting that I'm awake, and I watch his lips tilt up in a devious smile. I watch him as he starts to walk out of the ocean towards me, and I swear I don't know how to breathe for a moment. He's only wearing tight black shorts, and water drips all the way down his muscular form, between every muscle and groove, teasing me, I'm sure. His powerful thighs have him walking right up to me, and he crawls onto the sun lounger. Sea water drops onto my bare skin, my red bikini doing nothing to protect me from him.

Which is kinda the point.

"You're getting me wet," I tease. He laughs and shakes his hair, splashing me with water, and I giggle, pushing him away, but he is like a rock and moves nowhere. Maddox cups my cheek before kissing me softly.

"Did you sleep well?" he asks, looking down at me.

"Yes, and I saw her again. My grandmother," I say. "But I forgot to ask her name again. I feel like I'm never meant to know it."

"Perhaps not," he replies. "What did she tell you this time?"

I enjoy the fact this will surprise him. "That we would have a child with bright red hair and eyes of flames that look like yours. That we will have a child."

I ramble on as he doesn't say anything. "She said that it won't be long until he or she is here. Not right now, but in the next couple of years, perhaps… Say something."

He kisses me deeply and I moan, arching my body closer to his. "This is brilliant news, sweetheart."

"I think so too," I say. It's always been me who's more hesitant to have a child, and it's not from not wanting one, but more I wanted to make sure The Onyx was a safe place to bring a baby into. The truth is, it's been at peace for four years, and not much has changed. The people are happy, they adore us, and I know they would protect any child we had.

"I want to see what our child would be like, and I want to do it right. I see how Reign and Katy are with their children, the stark difference to how my father brought us up. He was cold and unfeeling, and there was no laughter, no joy, nothing. I like watching Reign chase his children around the castle, laughing as he hangs them over his shoulder and telling them their shit stick paintings are masterpieces. We always laugh around the dinner table, and it's filled with the opposite of what I was used to. I want all of it with you. I want that for our child, and I know that we can have that together. There might be more pressures with the crown and everything else that comes with it. But I want us to have that family, and I swear to you, I will be the best father I can be." He pauses with a smile. "I will love listening to them play violin as you try to teach them and we all go deaf in the meantime. I will love teaching my child to paint, even if they paint on every wall in the castle. I will read them a fairy tale every single night as I hold you both. I want all this, Riona."

Tears fill my eyes as I imagine it all with a small redheaded little girl. He will be an amazing father, I just know it. "I want that too."

In fact, hearing about the child that we will have makes me want to try for that child already, but maybe I can make that a surprise for us when we get home. I want our baby to be conceived in our home and born there too.

Maddox is already on the baby-making plan as he runs his hands down my arms, stomach and thighs.

"I have to tell you a secret first," I say, and he pauses.

"Have you been keeping secrets from me?" he asks, teasing. He knows the goddess told me something important, but it wasn't about me, and it was never the time to tell it.

"Ember is my sister," I say, and Maddox raises an eyebrow in surprise.

"Father's side, I presume?"

"Yes. One of the bastard children he had," I reply. "My grandmother whispered it to me. I won't meet the others, but she told me that Ember was the only one that I will meet in this lifetime and have a close connection to."

"So her adoptive dad is really her brother, and her queen is her sister. It also makes her a hellcaster princess by right," Maddox replies, thinking on it. "I can see why you kept this to yourself. It's complicated."

"I kept her as my ward to keep her close and to give her a place in the world that is right. She is a princess and should be in the royal family," I reply.

"Do you want to tell her?" he asks.

"Yes, I want to tell her when she is a bit older. I felt like she had a really messed up childhood, and things have only been normal for a short time. But she's older now, and I think it's probably about time I have a sit down and tell her the truth. I might tell Austin first, and we can tell her together."

Maddox nods in agreement. "He should be told first and Arlo too."

"Are you sticking up for your best friend?" I ask, referring to Austin.

Maddox pulls a face that is cute even when he isn't trying to be. "He's not my best friend."

I laugh because the truth is they really are best friends. They hated each other when they first met. But somehow, over these ten years, they have bonded. Ann and Katy are the women I'm closest to, and I consider them both my best friends. I miss Sophie, but she mourned me, moved on with her life and is happy now. It wouldn't be fair for me to turn up in her life. Truthfully, she is human, and she will die one day. Arlo was changed to a d'vampire eight years ago, and now all of us are going to live long lives, together, the way it should be.

"Oh, so you both love spending time together for no good reason?" I tease. "It's okay to have friends."

"He is a great help with the hellcasters," he replies, scowling. Austin loves to help us out with the more political side of running the island and to set himself up as almost like a people's person for the hellcasters and vampires who don't have a voice. He goes into the towns and villages to listen to what the people say and what they want, and retells that to Maddox and Reign in the meetings.

We can't change everything, but sometimes changing a little thing makes a big difference in the life of many. It all just works. The first time I realised Austin and Maddox were actually friends was six years ago when I found them both drunk and laughing about Reign's terrible attempt at a romantic gesture to Katy by singing through her labour.

Then it became a regular thing for Maddox and Austin to sit together, talking and drinking. They do like to drink together, and I kind of love to see my brother and mate being friendly. They fix each other with this friendship, and it was something Austin desperately needed as much as Maddox. Austin somehow got Maddox into actually having a friendship, something I never thought he would have.

Changing the subject, he tickles me for a bit until I beg him to stop, and we both lie down side by side, our faces close.

"Are we done with your trips?" he asks me. I nod. I made it my personal thing to give closure to all the families that I could find of humans taken in the auction. It started with me finding Lucy's boyfriend. I will never forget what Lucy asked me to do when we were on that boat traveling here together, and I always thought a part of her knew she was going to die right there and then in that cage. I promised her I would find him, and I did.

Lucy didn't give me much to go on, a beach house in California and a name, but I found him, and I went and told him everything. At first, he didn't quite believe me, and then Maddox showed him his fangs and a little orb of magic, and then he definitely did believe me. It turns out he'd been looking for her all this time. Never gave up, but he knew somewhere deep down that she wasn't here anymore. It's just it was hard to break his heart, but it was the right thing to do. I know Maddox regrets killing her, and he said sorry, but we both agreed not to tell her boyfriend that he did it.

He is human, and he couldn't understand Maddox if he tried.

I went down to all the humans and took over a year to make a very long list of anyone who knew anything about the families of the humans that have been killed. I made a list of over four hundred, and I found three hundred and sixty-two of them. The others, I will continue looking for, but I know there are thousands that will never get that closure. Never know what happened to their family members.

The only thing that I repeat to myself is that the auction is a horror of our past and will not be repeated. For now, we've still got people working on finding the others, and I hope that we do, but maybe they just can't be found. I sit up on my sun lounger and gather the towel underneath me to dry Maddox's hair. The towel is black, and it has our new royal crest in the middle.

We've gotten rid of the old crest, deciding that his father's rule and the crest that went with him just instilled fear in our people. We need to be fresh and new. So now there's a line of roses on a stem with thorns, a blue dagger and a black snake woven around the dagger in the shape of an infinity symbol. We think it represents everything to do with The Onyx and its mix of people under its rule. It represents freedom, a new way for our people. The snake is for the witches. The dagger is blue for the sirens. The roses represent the vampires, and the thorns are for the hellcasters.

Maddox brushes his hand down my cheek. "I know you're wishing you could find closure for all of them. If someone took you from me, I wouldn't stop searching the whole world. In fact, I'd just burn it all down for you in your memory, so they'd all know who you were and that you were gone. We can't change the past."

"Do you ever think about the people you killed?" I ask him. "I don't judge you for it. I know where you were and what was going on in your heart—"

He stops me and looks down for a second. "Yes, I do think about them sometimes. But I was a monster who was created, and I didn't know better. I was taught that was the only way, and I was taught that loving someone would kill that person. Quite truthfully, it nearly did. So I pushed everyone away, and I killed those that ever got close. I used and did whatever I could in my pain. The truth of all of it is, I just wish you were there sooner. My mate. I won't ever go back to that darkness."

I softly smile at him, loving his growth and the changes he has made to improve his outlook since we met. Who knew the villain could change and end up the good guy?

"Not unless someone threatens you, and then I will enjoy my old ways," he purrs with a dark undertone.

Not all that good.

I love him.

He is my villain, and I am his heart.

DESCRIPTION

I knew nothing about mates until the alpha rejected me...

Growing up in one of the biggest packs in the world, I have my life planned out for me from the second I turn eighteen and find my true mate in the moon ceremony.

Finding your true mate gives you the power to share the shifter energy they have, given to the males of the pack by the moon goddess herself.

The power to shift into a wolf.

But for the first time in the history of our pack, the new alpha is mated with a nobody. A foster kid living in the pack's orphanage with no ancestors or power to claim.

Me.

After being brutally rejected by my alpha mate, publicly humiliated and thrown away into the sea, the dark wolves of the Fall Mountain Pack find me.

They save me. The four alphas. The ones the world fears because of the darkness they live in. In their world? Being rejected is the only way to join their pack. The only way their lost and forbidden god gives them the power to shift without a mate.

I spent my life worshipping the moon goddess, when it turns out my life always belonged to another...

This is a full-length reverse harem romance novel full of sexy alpha males, steamy scenes, a strong heroine and a lot of sarcasm. Intended for 17+ readers. This is a trilogy.

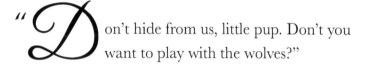 "**D**on't hide from us, little pup. Don't you want to play with the wolves?"

Beta Valeriu's voice rings out around me as I duck under the staircase of the empty house, dodging a few cobwebs that get trapped in my long blonde hair. Breathlessly, I sink to the floor and wrap my arms around my legs, trying not to breathe in the thick scent of damp and dust. Closing my eyes, I pray to the moon goddess that they will get bored with chasing me, but I know better. No goddess is going to save my ass tonight. Not when I'm being hunted by literal wolves.

I made a mistake. A big mistake. I went to a party in the pack, like all my other classmates at the beta's house, to celebrate the end of our schooling and, personally for me, turning eighteen. For some tiny reason, I thought I could be normal for one night. Be like them.

And not just one of the foster kids the pack keeps alive because of the laws put in place by a goddess no one has seen in hundreds of years. I should have known the betas in training would get drunk and decide chasing me for another one of their "fun" beatings would be a good way to prove themselves.

Wiping the blood from my bottom lip where one of them caught me in the forest with his fist, I stare at my blood-tipped fingers in a beam of moonlight shining through the broken panelled wall behind me.

I don't know why I think anyone is going to save me. I'm nothing to them, the pack, or to the moon goddess I pray to every night like everyone in this pack does.

The moon goddess hasn't saved me from shit.

Heavy footsteps echo closer, changing from crunching leaves to hitting concrete floor, and I know they are in the house now. A rat runs past my leg, and I nearly scream as I jolt backwards into a loose metal panel that vibrates, the metal smacking against another piece and revealing my location to the wolves hunting me.

Crap.

My hands shake as I climb to my feet and slowly step out into the middle of the room as Beta Valeriu comes in with his two sidekicks, who stumble to his side. I glance around the room, seeing the staircase is broken and there is an enormous gap on the second floor. It looks burnt out from a fire, but there is no other exit. I'm well and truly in trouble now. They stop in an intimidating line, all three of them muscular and jacked up enough to knock a car over. Their black hair is all the same shade, likely because they are all cousins, I'm sure, and they have deeply tanned skin that doesn't match how pale my skin is. Considering I'm a foster kid, I could have at least gotten the same looks as them, but oh no, the moon goddess gave me bright blonde hair that never stops growing fast and freckly pale skin to stand out. I look like the moon comparing itself to the beauty of the sun with everyone in my pack.

Beta Valeriu takes a long sip of his drink, his eyes flashing green, his wolf making it clear he likes the hunt. Valeriu is the newest beta, taking over from his father, who recently retired at two hundred years of age and gave the role to his son willingly. But Valeriu is a dick. Simple as. He might be good-looking, like most of the five betas are, but each one of them lacks a certain amount of brain cells. The thing is, wolves don't need to be smart to be betas, they just need the right bloodline and to kill when the alpha clicks his fingers.

All wolves like to hunt and kill. And damn, I'm always the hunted in this pack.

"You know better than to run from us, little Mairin. Little Mary the lamb who runs from the wolf," he sing songs the last part, taking a slow step forward, his shoe grating across the dirt under his feet. Always the height jokes with this tool. He might be over six foot, and sure, my five foot three height isn't intimidating, but has no one heard the phrase *small but deadly*?

Even if I'm not even a little deadly. "Who invited you to my party?"

"The entire class in our pack was invited," I bite out.

He laughs, the crisp sound echoing around me like a wave of frost. "We both know you might be in this pack, but that's only because of the law about killing female children. Otherwise, our alpha would have ripped you apart a long time ago."

Yeah, I know the law. The law that states female children cannot be killed because of the lack of female wolves born into the pack. There is roughly one female to five wolves in the pack, and it's been that way for a long time for who knows what reason. So, when they found me in the forest at twelve, with no memories and nearly dead, they had to take me in and save my life.

A life, they have reminded me daily, has only been given to me because of that law. The law doesn't stop the alpha from treating me like crap under his shoe or beating me close to death for shits and giggles. Only me, though. The other foster kid I live with is male, so he doesn't get the "special" attention I do. Thankfully.

"We both know you can't kill me or beat me bad enough to attract attention without the alpha here. So why don't you just walk away and find some poor dumbass girl to keep you busy at the party?" I blurt out, tired of all this. Tired of never saying what I want to these idiots and fearing the alpha all the time. A bitter laugh escapes Valeriu's mouth as his eyes fully glow this time. So do his friends', as I realise I just crossed a line with my smart-ass mouth.

My foster carer always said my mouth would get me into trouble.

Seems he is right once again.

A threatening growl explodes from Beta Valeriu's chest, making all the hairs on my arms stand up as I take a step back just as he shifts. I've seen it a million times, but it's always amazing and terrifying at the same time. Shifter energy, pure dark forest green magic, explodes around his body as he changes shape. The only sound in the room is his clicking bones and my heavy, panicked breathing as I search for a way out of here once again, even though I know it's pointless.

I've just wound up a wolf. A beta wolf, one of the most powerful in our pack.

Great job, Irin. Way to stay alive.

The shifter magic disappears, leaving a big white wolf in the space where Valeriu was. The wolf towers over me, like most of them do, and its head is huge enough to eat me with one bite. Just as he steps forward to jump, and I brace myself for something painful, a shadow of a man jumps down from the broken slats above me, landing with a thump. Dressed in a white cloak over jeans and a shirt, my foster carer completely blocks me from Valeriu's view, and I sigh in relief.

"I suggest you leave before I teach you what an experienced, albeit retired, beta wolf can do to a young pup like yourself. Trust me, it will hurt, and our alpha will look the other way."

The threat hangs in the air, spoken with an authority that Valeriu could never dream of having in his voice at eighteen years old. The room goes silent, filled with thick tension for a long time before I hear the wolf running off, followed by two pairs of footsteps moving quickly. My badass foster carer slowly turns around, lowering his hood and brushing his long grey hair back from his face. Smothered in wrinkles, Mike is ancient, and to this day, I have no clue why he offered to work with the foster kids of the pack. His blue eyes remind me of the pale sea I saw once when I was twelve. He always dresses like a Jedi from the human movies, in long cloaks and swords clipped to his hips that look like lightsabres as they glow with magic, and he tells me this is his personal style.

His name is even more human than most of the pack names that get regularly overused. My name, which is the only thing I know about my past thanks to a note in my hand, is as uncommon as it gets. According to an old book on names, it means Their Rebellion, which makes no sense. Mike is apparently a normal human name, and from the little interaction I've had with humans through their technology, his name couldn't be more common.

"You are extremely lucky my back was playing up and I went for a walk, Irin," he sternly comments, and I sigh.

"I'm sorry," I reply, knowing there isn't much else I can say at this point. "The mating ceremony is tomorrow, and I wanted one night of being normal. I shouldn't have snuck out of the foster house."

"No, you should not have when your freedom is so close," he counters and reaches up, gently pinching my chin with his fingers and turning my head to the side. "Your lip is cut, and there is considerable bruising to your cheek. Do you like being beaten by those pups?"

"No, of course not," I say, tugging my face away, still tasting my blood in my mouth. "I wanted to be normal! Why is that so much to ask?"

"Normal is for humans and not shifters. It is why they gave us the United Kingdom and Ireland and then made walls around the islands to stop us from getting out. They want normal, and we need nothing more than what is here: our pack," he begins, telling me what I already know. They agreed three hundred years ago we would take this part of earth as our own, and the humans had the rest. No one wanted interbreeding, and this was the best way to keep peace. So the United Kingdom's lands were separated into four packs. One in England, one in Wales, one in Scotland and one in Ireland. Now there are just two packs, thanks to the shifter wars: the Ravensword Pack that is my home, who worship the moon goddess, and then the Fall Mountain Pack, who owns Ireland, a pack we are always at war with. Whoever they worship, it isn't our goddess, and everything I know about them suggests they are brutal. Unfeeling. Cruel.

Which is exactly why I've never tried to leave my pack to go there. It might be shit here, but at least it's kind of safe and I have a future. Of sorts.

"Do you think it will be better for me when I find my mate tomorrow?" I question…not that I want a mate who will control me with his shifter energy. But it means I will shift into a wolf, like every female can when they are mated, and I've always wanted that.

Plus, a tiny part of me wants to know who the moon goddess herself has chosen for me. The other half of my soul. My true mate. Someone who won't see me as the foster kid who has no family, and will just want me.

Mike looks down at me, and something unreadable crosses his eyes. He turns away and starts walking out of the abandoned house, and I jog to catch up with him. Snowflakes drop into my blonde hair as we head through the forest, back to the foster home, the place I will finally leave one way or another tomorrow. I pull my leather jacket around my chest, over my brown T-shirt for warmth. My torn and worn out jeans are soaked with snow after a few minutes of walking, the snow becoming thicker with every minute. Mike is silent as we walk past the rocks that mark the small pathway until we get to the top of the hill that overlooks the main pack city of Ravensword.

Towering buildings line the River Thames that flows through the middle of the city. The bright lights make it look like a reflection of the stars in the sky, and the sight is beautiful. It might be a messed up place, but I can't help but admire it. I remember the first time I saw the city from here, a few days after I was found and healed. I remember thinking I had woken up from hell to see heaven, but soon I learnt heaven was too nice of a word for this place. The night is silent up here, missing the usual noise of the people in the city, and I silently stare down wondering why we have stopped.

"What do you see when you look at the city, Irin?"

I blow out a long breath. "Somewhere I need to escape."

I don't see his disappointment, but I easily feel it.

"I see my home, a place with darkness in its corners but so much light. I see a place even a foster wolf with no family or ancestors to call on can find happiness tomorrow," he responds. "Stop looking at the stars for your escape, Irin, because tomorrow you will find your home in the city you are trying so hard to see nothing but darkness in."

He carries on walking, and I follow behind him, trying to do what he has asked, but within seconds my eyes drift up to the stars once again.

Because Mike is right, I am always looking for my way to escape, and I always will. I wasn't born in this pack, and I came from outside the walls that have been up for hundreds of years. That's the only explanation for how they found me in a forest with nothing more than a small glass bottle in my hand and a note with my name on it. No one knows how that is possible, least of all me, but somehow I'm going to figure it out. I have to.

Read more here…

PART I

DESCRIPTION

The alpha of hell is my fated mate and he rejected me.

I'm an outcast in my pack and have been since

the day I was born. Shunned by most of the wolves around me, I've managed to stay out of trouble… until now.

Now The Alpha of Stormfire is hunting me, but he doesn't want to claim me as his mate.

He wants me dead.

Forced to leave my old life behind, I have no choice but to go on the run. Luckily, The Demon Hunting Trials is the perfect place to hide, even if it comes with a few obstacles.

Such as their leader is a total jerk, a wolf is blackmailing me to be his friend, and I swear my new, sexy as sin partner is trying to get us killed.

With demons running amok and the alpha of hell searching for me, I hope I can live long enough to get my revenge.

18+ Dark reverse harem romance full with a sassy and sarcastic heroine who finds her match.

There isn't enough booze in the shifter world to deal with alpha egos.

I take a deep drink of the red wine I stole from the teacher's lounge at Caeli Pack Academy before passing it to my best friend. The only person in the whole world (okay, just the academy) who I like. She's also the sole reason the alpha's sons are walking right over to us at this lame excuse for a party to celebrate the rare blood moon. Who throws a party for eighteen-year-olds without booze?

Aurelia Winters coughs as she takes a long drink and rolls her eyes at me when I chuckle. Although she tends to think otherwise, Aurelia is ridiculously stunning, and it's mostly down to her bloodline. She looks just like her mum, but her father's genes are strong and make her the perfect example of a Caeli wolf. Taking another sip from the bottle, Aurelia tucks her curly blonde hair behind her ears and looks past me at the alpha's sons with her big blue eyes. She is the perfect wolf at the Caeli Pack Academy, whereas me, on the other hand, I stand out as the outcast they put up with. I'm a red in a world of white with my dark-red hair and red-furred wolf. Other than the streak of white hair that falls down the side of my cheek, there isn't much about me that lets me mix in with the pack I have always lived in.

The Caeli Pack is hidden deep in the snowy Mountains of Alaska, where no one ever comes because it's too high up and the humans are afraid of us. Mostly because we're supernatural beings who don't mix well with them since they only see us as a means to protect them from the bad things in the world. Every pack in the world has its mission, its purpose, and Caeli's is learning and recording every event in the world of shifters. Basically, librarians with a bite.

"I stand out everywhere," I mutter to Aurelia.

"So? You're pretty and unusual here. That's not a bad thing," she replies. "Don't worry so much."

Says the girl who fits into our pack better than my ass fits into these skinny jeans. I don't hide or blend in very well. Aurelia is the opposite. At least, she is until we're at a party like this where she stands out far more than I do in some sense. It's all because of the mating season. In a year's time, most females will have chosen a mate, and the males all want the prettiest wolf in the pack which is Aurelia.

Finding a mate is definitely not on my to-do list. At least not with any of these wolves.

I take the bottle from Aurelia. "I think I should just leave at the end of the academy year in two weeks. Maybe join the demon-hunting trials in the Stormfire pack or something." Throwing back a deep mouthful, I wipe my lips with the back of my hand. "Hell, maybe I could look for my father and actually fit in there."

Aurelia gawks at me, then snatches the bottle. "Are you freaking crazy? You could also die in the trials. That's it. No more booze for you."

I glare at her jokingly. "Hey, I'm not even tipsy!"

"You're speaking like my aunt on New Year's Eve! Have you forgotten that you could get killed trying to capture those disgusting demons? They eat wolves for fun. Why would you even want that?" She shakes her head. "You're safe here. You shouldn't leave."

"My brother left."

With a sigh, she rests her head on my shoulder for a few seconds. "But he's a male and strong. There are like three female demon hunters in the whole of the Stormfire pack, and each of them are totally badass."

"So you're saying I'm not a badass?" I question with a raised eyebrow.

She laughs. "If you were brought up in Stormfire, taught to fight from a kid instead of how to read a book and study like our pack taught, we might be having a different conversation. But your circumstances are totally different. You were brought up a Caeli, and we both don't have a clue about fighting demons or capturing them. Come on, Lilith. You know this. Please tell me you weren't being serious?"

I don't answer her because I know she's right. But the thought of studying wolf history and doing nothing more than studying for the rest of my life makes me feel sick. It's like my pack is squeezing the life out of me with each passing day, and the only way to stop is to find an escape.

"We can talk about it later," I say, shrugging my shoulder. "They are nearly here."

Aurelia raises her head and straightens her tight, sparkling yellow dress that shows off her long legs. I cross my own covered legs, the movement straining my jeans and knocking mud off my heavy boots. Aurelia decided that we both needed to dress up and come to this party at one of her friend's houses, something that I would never attend before now because honestly, parties are not my thing. I'd much rather be drinking this bottle of red wine on my own back in my room, but I can't always be unsociable when my best friend is a big extrovert. I need to compromise sometimes, even if that means leaving my bedroom. C'est la vie, right?

The alpha sons stomp over from the dance floor that we can see at the end of the corridor we are sitting in. The blasting music vibrates through the room, shaking the floor almost from the noise of it, and pop song comes on that sings about humans shaking their asses. Another reason I tend to avoid these things. Why does the music always suck? I'd much rather they played some rock. Hell, if they put on some Guns N' Roses, I might even bust some real moves. None of this swaying, grinding nonsense.

Beside me, a dancing Aurelia knocks my shoulder as she sings the song word for word. I can't help but smile at her. I thought I could hide back here with her, but now the alpha's twin sons' shadows hang over us, I'm thinking my hiding skills need work.

This was a really bad idea.

They're both looking at her like she's the answer to their prayers, the very air to their lungs, while their mating scent invades my own lungs so much that I nearly gag. They never stop staring at Aurelia even as they finally come to a stop, and I know why. Everyone knows she's going to be an alpha female at some point because her wolf is strong, a born leader, and her human incomparably beautiful.

All the things you need to be on the alpha's sons' radar.

As for me? Everyone knows I'm only ever going to be the outcast. It's because I really, really don't belong in this pack. Caeli is all about reputation and utmost control, of unrivalled intellect and centuries-old knowledge that are the very bones of our existence. Each pack in our world has its own unique purpose. Caeli's is record-keeping and the continuous search for better, more proficient pack medicine; something that has been installed into me since I was a pup.

Learn for the Pack—the motto every wolf here lives by.

Every wolf except for me.

As my mum puts it, I've always been too wild, too uncontrollable, and in general too nosy for my own good. I'm sure that's the sole reason most of the teachers at this academy absolutely hate me and most likely the reason that my adopted brother sometimes pretends I'm not really his sister. Being an embarrassment to the shifter world is weirdly something I can live with. But being an embarrassment to my own family is the only thing that's kept me from running away.

Damn, I need more wine if I'm going to think about my family.

The alpha's sons, Dumb and Dumber as I've nicknamed them, just gaze with wide eyes at Aurelia. Their expressions are almost panicked. Aurelia watches back and sighs. It always makes me laugh how the simple fact she stares down future alphas who will no doubt one day fight for the chance to be pack leader, and subsequently, choose her as the alpha female if she chooses them, too. But I don't know if she will. Aurelia is picky about her guys, a lot like me. Not that many have been interested in the girl who doesn't belong here. Beyond their curiosity, I'm usually too different for them to look at twice.

The alpha sons may be handsome and muscular, both of them built like dump trucks, but for as strong as they are, there's not a lot going on upstairs under their thick, white-blond hair. My point is proven when they both stumble for a second on what to say to Aurelia. They scratch their heads, no doubt in search of a cheesy, over-thought chat-up line, and then one of them says something that surprises even me a little.

"Would you like to come and dance to the song that is playing? I heard you say it was your favourite once."

And for whatever reason in the world, Aurelia appears almost happy that one of them noticed she likes the song that's playing.

She looks at me, and I nod. "Go. I'm going back to my room with the wine."

"Okay, see you back there later," she replies with a big smile.

The two of them quickly wander off down the corridor, and I hear her laugh a while later as I take another long drink of the bottle. A warm buzz floats down my body, the wine finally kicking in, but then I notice I'm left alone with the other alpha's son who I can never remember the name of. Every girl at this academy, other than me and Aurelia, has got their names memorised and written down in their diaries with love hearts. I know she doesn't do silly stuff like that just because we share a room and have done since we both came here when we were eight, like every young pack member. Their names come back to me now I gaze at them; Mathi and… Dammit, I can't remember what the other one's name is.

I stand and fake a big yawn before trying to walk away. But Mathi reaches out and grabs my arm, stopping me. I knew it was never going to be that easy. These alpha-holes rarely ever take a hint.

I narrow my eyes on his brown ones, a big contrast to my light grey. "Let. Go."

A smirk slides over his lips. "No. Why should I?"

He moves closer to me, lining up our bodies, and the disgusting thoughts circling in his head are written on his face as clear as day. This asshole better back off. He can't touch me; his father himself accepted me into the pack, which means I have the alpha's protection until he isn't alpha anymore. Of course, I worry about what will happen to me if the next alpha, AKA Dumb or his brother, Dumber, become alpha. But that won't be for some time yet. Right now, my focus is to get this unwanted paw off my body.

At the sight of me trying to wiggle my arm free, his smirk deepens into a malicious smile. He tightens his grip and pulls me closer, bringing his lips to my ear.

"You and I both know no one would notice if you went missing. You are just the outcast, the red wolf in a pack of white purebreds." He jolts me harder against him, his hands leaving bruises on my arm, but I refuse to turn away, to even wince at the pain. "Actually, that begs the question as to why you are still here. I'm surprised my father let you into the academy at all, half-breed."

Searing rage slams into me at the insult. Half-breed is the delightful nickname purebreds use for wolves like me; a subtle reminder of our so-called inferiority. Well, that's what they like to think. Anyone who's called me a half-breed usually walks away with a black eye.

I ball my hands into fists. "Maybe your dear father likes my mum a little too much. He does always seem to be admiring her."

The wolf's smile fades, and I inwardly chuckle at his stupid expression. So easily provoked, these young alphas. However, my satisfaction is short-lived. With a growl, he slams me into the wall, and I gasp from the impact. He presses his thick forearm against my neck, holding me in place, and the air dies in my lungs.

"Is that... any way... to treat a lady?" I choke out, unsure why I'm using my last breaths to anger him further. Then again, the fury burning on his gaze does make my sacrifice worth it. Besides, it's not like I'm unused to assholes like this one asserting their authority over me. Alphas love putting unruly wolves like me in their place.

Too bad I've never quite learned how to stay in mine.

Despite the black spots seeping into my vision, I stare up at him, wondering what exactly he's going to do. One thing is for sure—this dickwad has solidified my desire to leave his pack as soon as possible. I'll never follow an alpha who treats their packmates this way.

"Do you want to die, half-breed?" he growls.

I resist the urge to give him a sarcastic reply. I may be brave, but as my brother puts it, I can be pretty stupidly brave.

And I know that challenging an alpha son is really not a good idea.

I might be able to fight well, thanks to all the training the Academy has taught me. But even I know that you can't beat a guy twice your size in a small corridor like this, with no weapons on me, and his forearm pressed on my windpipe.

He gazes down at me and raises an eyebrow, but something burns on my arm.

In the corner of my eye, my wolf mark in the middle of my arm burns vividly. The swirls that form a wolf shape glow a deep, vibrant red, at first burning painfully but they quickly fade into a dull ache that fills my entire body.

Mathi follows my gaze to the mark and smiles.

"Seems like your parents are calling you home," he snarls, loosening the pressure on my throat. "Did your mum's mate ever realise that you weren't his?"

This asshole knows damn well my dad knows I'm not his. I was conceived and born before my mum ever mated. Everyone in the pack knows it. It was a big scandal, and to this day I still hear the boring wolves talking about it. Caeli wolves love to gossip because they have nothing better to do.

I grit my teeth at the jab. "Fuck. Off."

He raises his free hand as if to strike me. I don't flinch, and that seems to piss him off. He grabs me by the scruff of the neck and slams me against the wall again, drawing everyone's attention.

"Go back to your little family, half-breed. But just remember that when I'm alpha, your kind will never be welcome here." He releases me with a derisive scoff. "Off you go now, run back home."

I don't reply despite the tinge of fear that his threat elicits in me. My wolf, however, bares her teeth and snaps her jaw at him in retaliation. I need to get out of here before I shift and try to take on an alpha twice my size. The fading burn from my family's mark sears in my mind, screaming down to my soul for me to move.

Biting back my spiteful retort, I jog down the corridor and take a left out of the noisy house, dodging students who whistle and tease me. The cool night air lifts my hair over my shoulders when I step onto the porch. I take a deep breath and jog into the snowy outskirts that surround the house. Snow-capped trees line the distance, and I make a break for them. The cold doesn't bother me, even when I duck behind a tree and strip off. Once I'm fully naked, I bundle my clothes into a ball and shove them into the small bag I always carry with me.

I rest my head against the tree and gaze up at the moon cutting through the frozen leaves. My breath comes out in puffs of smoke, and for a moment I stay there, thinking about how much

I'd have liked to punch that alpha-hole in the throat.

But my family needs me.

I dig my feet into the earth and arch forward, spreading my fingers through the snow. Shifting is an effortless, painless task for me, almost like breathing. I transform into my wolf easily, letting my body change until my red paws sink into the ground. Picking the bag up with my fangs, I run through the forest back towards the towering academy hidden in a clearing shrouded in blankets of untouched snow. It's eerily silent at this time of night. Most people are sleeping, and those who find themselves awake under the light of the moon, venture into the woods to hunt.

The side door of the academy is always left open, and I slip through it. The wood corridors echo every hit of my wolf's claws on them as we dodge around corridors of lockers. We keep running until we get to the main stairs and head straight up to our room and pause. My wolf drops my bag on the floor, and we use our advanced hearing to make sure no one is around before shifting back. Most wolves don't care about nudity, but I'm not one of them.

I unlock my door and head inside with my bag, quickly getting back into my jeans, plain black tee-shirt and boots. I search the messy floor for my phone next. I push a few items of clothing around before I find it and try ringing my parents, but it goes straight to voicemail. I ring my adopted elder brother, but again, straight to voicemail. My family are bloody useless with phones. Instead of trying to keep ringing them, I decide I might as well just go and see them since it's not too far to walk. It's a weird thing for them to use a wolf call with my mark, but I'm sure everything is fine, even if something in the back of my mind doesn't think so. My mum never uses the mark to summon me, and my dad definitely hasn't done it. He likes to pretend I don't exist. That only leaves my brother, but Leo's too busy working as a new demon hunter to bother summoning me. I guess there's only one way to get to the bottom of this.

Time to go home and see what the hell is going on.

ALPHA HELL (THE REJECTED MATE SERIES #1)…

CHAPTER TWO

LILITH THORNBLOOD

Burning leaves.

It's all I can smell when I emerge from the trees surrounding my childhood home. The scent clings to my snow-covered fur and permeates the night air like a sceptic perfume. I pause on the outskirts of the forest and lift my head towards the sky. A stiff breeze sweeps over me and carries the scent downwind, meaning it's coming from the direction of my house.

The scent can only belong to a Stormfire wolf, but why would one of them trespass into our territory? Unless my parents invited them. Could that be why I've been summoned?

I slip out of the trees and run across the field towards my home. The three-storey, red-brick building has been in my family for generations. The slanted roof is covered in a thick blanket of snow, and icicles dangle from the gutters to overshadow the wooden porch. My dad's car is parked in the driveway, and the shed, which we use for shifting, has been left open.

Slowing my gait, I scan the ground. Fresh paw prints. They're triple the size of my own when I step into them. I take a cautious sniff, and sure enough, burning leaves cling to the indentations.

I hurry into the shed and shift back. Rummaging through my bag, I dress quickly, lock the door behind me, and climb the porch steps. Only the kitchen light is on. Mum must be cooking dinner. My stomach clenches, and a feeling of dread washes over me when I touch the door.

Someone with magic has been there. The only creatures who can use magic nowadays are demons. Not even the headmaster at the academy is able to cast spells; he has to summon a demon to do it for him.

I take a deep breath and open the front door. One step, two steps over the threshold, and my heart clenches at what I see inside our little kitchen. My mother, held by the throat by the largest man I've ever seen, and my father standing beside her as pale as a ghost. The unfamiliar male towers several feet above the both of them, and his grasp on my mum's throat.

"Welcome home, Lilith Thornblood."

His deep, powerful voice sends a shiver running down the length of my spine. He's completely naked from the waist up. His torso is covered in symbolic tattoos the same black colour as his hair. Thick gold bands encircle his arms, and a black medallion with a ruby centre hands around his neck. The jewel glows just like his crimson eyes, all of them cutting into me like molten shards.

"I believe introductions are in order," he says, flashing the tip of his fangs in a smile that doesn't reach his eyes.

My mother's wide, terrified ones never leave my face. It kills me to see her so afraid. Even my dad has cowered a little in size; a gesture meant to convey submission in the presence of an alpha.

"I know who you are."

He lifts a scarred brow. "Oh?"

I peel my gaze from the hand on my mother's throat to glare at him. "You're the alpha of Stormfire. You guard the Gates of Hell. Apparently, you have quite the temper and once wiped out an entire pack just because their alpha stole from you."

The alpha inclines his head. "The very one."

He regards me through the barest slits of his eyes. A minute shake of his head threatens disappointment as he looks at me. Look isn't quite the right word. The Stormfire alpha is dissecting me into pieces, stripping me naked with his gaze until I'm only flesh and blood. From his stony expression, I appeal less to him than a mildly interesting object, and for some insane reason it raises my hackles.

Despite everything my parents and pack have taught me, I make a point of holding the alpha's gaze as boldly and firmly as he holds mine. "What do you want?" I practically spit out at him.

My dad crosses the length of the kitchen and slaps me so quickly I stumble back in surprise, my body thudding into the back of the door. I'm used to his temper, and his fists, but still, I didn't expect this hit.

"Show the alpha some goddamn respect!"

The impact forces me to break eye contact, but not before I catch sight of the alpha's eyes glowing a deep shade of black.

"Touch her again and you'll lose more than a hand." He adds just the slightest bit of pressure to my mum's throat, and the tips of his claws dent her skin.

She doesn't so much as draw a single breath. Dad takes a big step back from me in fear for my mum, his mate's, life.

The alpha cuts his gaze to me. "Come."

He drags my mum from the kitchen, and my dad slowly takes up the rear, his expression a little grimmer than before. My heart thrashes so violently I can scarcely make out their footsteps as they head into the dining room. For a moment I just stand there in the kitchen, and then I follow suit, each step laced with a growing, burning hatred for this alpha. And my dad. Why is he letting this alpha treat my mum this way? It's almost like he couldn't care less about her. While he's always been like that towards me, he's never disrespected my mum. I don't even care if he's only doing it because there's an alpha in our home. It's unacceptable.

If my mum didn't appear so terrified in the alpha's presence, I'd grab a knife from the kitchen and swing at the alpha, then I'd take my mum away where my dad can never find her again. She's always deserved better than him.

We both deserve better.

Once I reach our open-plan living room, everyone is seated at the dining table; the alpha where my dad would usually sit, my mum beside him. I sweep my gaze over the surface, unsurprised to find it set for only one. Of course the alpha would eat before any of us. It's customary in packs that alphas should eat first and, usually, alone. With a wave of his tattooed hand, a thin chain slithers around my mum's wrist. It wraps around the table leg, binding her to the alpha's side. She glances at me standing in the doorway, her eyes wide and stark with fear, and more searing-hot fury consumes me.

The alpha pulls out a chair and gestures to it dismissively. "By all means, have a seat."

Everything about this male pisses me off. From the arrogant way he struts around my home like he owns it, to the manner in which he curls the edge of his lips and looks at me like I'm a piece of meat… So typical of every other alpha out there, and yet so, so much worse.

He doesn't even wait to see if I'll obey his command. With not a care in the world, he claims the seat at the other end of the table and reaches for the bottle of red wine. My dad sits across from my mum, leaving only the pulled-out chair at the end for me. My every instinct screams to shift and challenge this alpha, but I'm not an idiot. Not only does he hold my mother prisoner, but I'm willing to bet his wolf is three times the size of mine. I'd be dead before I could so much as sink my teeth into his throat.

There's really nothing for it. If I'm to figure out what the hell is going on and get my parents out of this alive, I need to play nicely; something I've failed to do so far in my eighteen years.

I settle down on the opposite side. The silence is so tense I could cut it with the alpha's butterknife. Instead, I lift my eyes from the polished surface of the table and look at him.

"Why are you here?" I repeat, ensuring my voice is firm. "And what do you want?"

My dad slams his fist on the table and prepares to stand. "Dammit, child! How many times have I told you? Do not speak unless spoken—"

The alpha's voice stops him. Dad freezes in his half-crouched position, and his worried eyes flick to the other end of the table.

"You'd do well to follow your own advice, Valerio." The alpha narrows his eyes on me. "At any rate, I see no problem in answering her questions. She is my mate, is she not?"

CHAPTER THREE

LILITH THORNBLOOD

It's clearly a rhetorical question, one that sends my heart shooting to the pit of my stomach. Did he just say what I think he did? My pulse skyrockets, and I clench my hands underneath the table. For the first time since entering the dining room, my mother isn't looking at me. It's as if she can't bring herself to. I've never seen my mum as anything but the beautiful and graceful wolf with long white hair I wish I had. I can't ever remember seeing my mum scared or weak. I know her expression scares me far more than the alpha behind her and calling me his mate could ever do.

"I'm here to collect what's mine." The alpha pours himself a glass of wine and sniffs the contents before taking a sip. His eyes cut over the glass to me. "That would be you."

A nervous laugh bubbles in my chest and quickly escapes my lips. "W-what? You can't be serious?" I glance at my mum, my chest rising unevenly. "Mum, what the hell is going on?"

But she doesn't say a word. The colour has completely drained from her face. She seems like she's about to be sick.

"One thing you should know about me, little mate," the alpha says in a dangerously low voice, dragging my attention back to him, "is that I am only ever serious. You belong to me and you are my fated mate. The Crescent Mother wills it."

The glimmer of anxiety that had gripped me a moment ago vanishes, replaced with more searing-hot anger.

"I don't belong to anyone," I spit back at him. "Especially not a wolf who came here uninvited and raised his own hands to my mother!"

He picks up my mum's favourite cutlery and begins cutting his meat. "Who says I came here uninvited?"

My dad shifts nervously, and my mum's face turns a violent shade of red. This doesn't make any sense. If they invited him, why would he threaten to hurt my mum? There's no way my mum would invite the alpha of another pack to our home. It's unheard of unless it's to the house of another alpha. And as much as my dad likes to pretend he's an alpha behind closed doors, he's nothing of the sort.

I straighten. "I don't know how things work in your pack, *Alpha*, but shackling your host to a table isn't something we do in Caeli."

He chuckles and shoves a slice of meat into his mouth. "You've got fire in you, little mate. Good. You'll need it when I take you home."

"*This* is my home," I snarl at him.

The alpha dismisses my retort and continues eating. "I see your mother failed to inform you of your situation. Allow me to explain." He wipes his mouth with a silk handkerchief and then tosses it on his near empty plate. "Eighteen years ago, your mother and I came to an agreement. In exchange for helping her flee a rather complicated situation, your mother promised me a mate worthy of the Stormfire alpha. I've come to see just how worthy of a mate you truly are."

The air clamps in my chest. It's like the alpha has thrust a paw into my chest and is squeezing my heart with his razor-sharp claws. Through the tears blurring my vision, I glare venomously at my dad. He used to say there would come a day when my past would catch up with me. Until this very moment, I never understood what he meant. But it was that I'd been promised to an alpha who would one day come to collect me. And he knew.

My *mum* knew.

I wonder if my brother and Aurelia were aware, too.

The thought twists my stomach into a pile of knots, and a rush of anxiety trickles down my spine. This can't really be happening. It's like I've fallen through a portal to an alternative universe where my own family would betray me. I glance at my mum, searching for something, anything, that will tell me the alpha is lying. But she only looks away as her lower lip trembles. She really did do it.

My mum promised me to an alpha when I was just a baby.

I snap my head to the alpha in question and glare at him. He just fucking smirks at me like this is an amusing game to him. But then something changes. His lips thin, and he sniffs the air. His prior amusement melts from his countenance like wet snow, and he rises from the table. Slowly, he comes towards me, and I struggle to hold his gaze this time. There's something darker about it, something primal and deadly. Power radiates off him like an all-encompassing shadow. His presence alone swallows up everything in the room, and despite my best efforts, I shrink a little in my chair.

He stops beside me and picks up a strand of my long, auburn hair. A muscle ticks in his jaw, and a crease forms between his brows when he lifts the strand to smell it. His eyes darken into a deeper onyx. Faster than I can blink, he leans forward and brushes his fangs along my neck. I grip my thighs and close my eyes. I know what he's doing. He's taking in my scent to see whether or not I'm 'worthy' of him. From the way my palms turn sweaty and my heart convulses, he can no doubt smell the whirlwind of emotions wreaking havoc within me.

"You smell of weakness," he breathes, the tip of his fangs sweeping over the pulse in the side of my throat. "Weak wolves do not belong in my pack."

"My daughter is a lot of things, Rizer. A half-breed and nuisance, sure, but no wolf of my line has ever been weak," my dad says.

In my shock, I open my eyes to gawk at him. I've never heard him defend me like this before. Even when our own pack ridiculed me, he said nothing.

Did nothing.

A foolish part of me actually hopes to find compassion when I face him, but there's only that same old, familiar coldness. I wish I knew what I did to make him despise me so much. The fact that he just said I'm part of 'his' line means he does see me as part of the Valerio family, so it can't be that I'm not his biological kid.

"Your line is also descended from cowards and liars," Rizer growls, moving behind me.

Again he sniffs my hair, and I dig my fingernails into my jeans. My mother holds my gaze, but ever so quickly, she glances at the front door.

"That I could ignore. But weakness? That is disgusting and cannot be tolerated. You should not be allowed to exist."

I swallow the nervous lump in my throat and watch my mother drape her free hand over the alpha's knife. Her glancing at the front door was a signal for me to run. But I can't just run while she's chained to the table. However, before I can so much as protest, she throws the wine glass onto the table. The glass smashing against the wooden floor rouses the alpha's attention, if just for a second. That's all I need to jump up from the table and out of the way, moments before the knife whistles through the air towards the alpha.

The blade pierces him in the chest, and for a second, he just stands next to me, his eyes wide.

"*What have you done?*" My dad's chair falls over and he shoots up from his chair. He rushes over to the alpha and stumbles to his knees beside him. Shaking hands hover over the dead body, but they can't quite bring themselves to touch the bloodstains on his chest. Unfortunately, the alpha won't remain dead for long; alphas always regenerate, usually once the source of their death has been removed from their body, but there's rumours that alphas don't require that.

I doubt a knife to the heart will keep Rizer dead for long.

"He'll kill us," my dad chokes out, his hands trembling so violently his whole upper body shakes. "He'll kill us all!"

My mum doesn't even glance at him. "Lilith, go. We don't have long."

Blood pounds in my head and I shake it in disbelief. "The chain—"

"Go without me!"

I flinch at the volume of her tone but keep shaking my head. "N-no, I can't. I'm not leaving you here, Mum!"

As I rush over to her side, my dad continues muttering about how the alpha will kill us—him—once he wakes up. He really is a coward. I'm glad he's not my real dad. Once I reach my mum and look down at the chain cutting into her skin, the tears I've been struggling to hold back finally fall from my lashes. She follows my gaze, and instead of being scared or upset, she just smiles at me. Slowly, she tucks my hair behind my ear and pats my head like she's done since I was a kid.

"Don't worry, sweetie, I'll be right behind you." And with that, she pushes me towards the front door, her chain scraping the table. "Take the backpack hanging by the door and go. Don't turn back. I love you, baby."

A sob bursts from my trembling lips. "I love you, too, Mum."

I quickly hug her, grab the bag, and then I'm taking off through the front door without so much as a glance at my dad.

My boots barely hit the ground when I shift into my wolf, take the bag into my mouth, and run. I never feel the cold, but right now I'm as cold as the snow crunching beneath my paws. My breath streams out in harsh, rapid puffs but I head into the trees as fast I've ever ran in my life, not even bothering to bring my clothes. I keep going until a deafening howl cuts through the air in the distance and my fur instantly stands on end.

Rizer.

His burning-leaves scent carries on the downwind, and my stomach roils with a mixture of fear and anger. I pause by a frozen creek and stare down at my reflection on the icy surface. My wolf looks as dejected as I feel. Did my mum even make it like she said she would? A small part of me hopes she did and that I'll see her soon, that she will catch up with me. But the rest of me, no matter how much I want to refute it, shatters as if I knew all along: my mum was never getting out of that house alive.

A sick, twisted piece of me hopes my dad never made it out. He'd been perfectly willing to hand me over to the alpha like a bit of discarded meat. My mum had been nothing but terrified from the moment I entered the kitchen. My eyes water at the thought of her, but I quickly push them aside and continue. There will be time to mourn for her later. I need to get out of here before the alpha catches up with me.

With this shadowing over me, I run faster through the forest. It's a little ironic that I've spent my childhood exploring these woods. I know every tree, every creek and clearing, and yet I don't know where to go. I could go back to the party and get Aurelia, then come up with a plan. But I don't want to drag her into this. My best option would be to seek refuge in the academy. That means going east.

Another howl echoes in the near distance, followed by another. Their cadence is so different to what I'm used to hearing amongst Caeli wolves, which means these ones aren't part of my pack. They must be from Stormfire. Damn it! They've blocked out the academy. West will just take me to Aurelia, and I don't want to endanger her. All I can do is head north in hopes that I find a place good enough to hide.

After hours of running, my limbs ache from exertion, and I have no choice but to stop to rest. The Stormfire howls stopped about a mile back. I'm not stupid enough to think they've given up hunting me. Leaning against a tree, I glance up at the bloodstained moon, and a powerful urge to howl at her fullness consumes me. My mum used to say that the Crescent Mother was more likely to bless her wolves on the night of a full moon. It's a slim chance, but right now, I'll do anything to get out of here.

I need your help. Please tell me where I should go. Give me a sign. Please. Something. Crescent Mother, help me.

In answer to my prayer is the cloying smell of more burning leaves, and the low grumble of a howl rumbling in the back of a wolf's throat. I whip my head around in search of the wolf. Through the shadowy trees, I'm able to decipher an enormous red wolf surrounded in tendrils of smoke. The medallion around its powerful neck gleams in the moonlight.

Uhh, Crescent Mother… This isn't what I quite had in mind.

Rizer snaps his bloody jaw at me and takes a step. The blood on his lips carries my mum's scent. A low whimper escapes me, and I instinctively back away from him. I lower my head and press my tail tightly between my hind legs. More howls resonate close by. There's no way I'll be able to fight off Rizer let alone the others.

In the corner of my eye, a light flickers in the darkness around me. The bright glow pulls me towards it like gravity. I turn my head ever so slightly, and relief washes over me. A huge staircase stands proudly on the forest floor, and right at the top is a bright orange light.

A portal.

I don't even stop to question where it might lead me.

I charge up the stairs and dive head-first into the blinding, beautiful light.

LILITH THORNBLOOD

CHAPTER FOUR

LILITH THORNBLOOD

I *really* hate portals.

I stumble through the light, my stomach feeling like a thousand bees are bouncing around in it, and smack hard into the stairs on the other side. I stand, my wolf shaking our head, just as the edge of the old, cracked steps to the portal gives way under my feet.

My wolf whines as we fall down the steps, right off a damn cliff of all things. My body smacks across the rock side, sharp pebbles digging into my calves. My wolf tries to dig its claws into the cliffside to stop us. Roots and branches snag in my fur and against my legs as I keep falling, unable to find anything to stop us. I briefly see everything is red and burning right before I crash into something that instantly burns my back.

Standing quickly, I move off the tiny pool of lava under me, letting my wolf heal the brief burns. Breathlessly, I take a second to glance around me and I freeze. My blood runs cold when I realise exactly where I am.

The Stormfire pack.

Also known as—Hell itself.

What the hell? I'm not even on Earth anymore.

In my horror, I look up at the portal on top of the mountain, wondering why the alpha isn't right on my heels. He should be able to follow me.

This is his frigging pack, after all.

Shit. Shit. Shit.

My brother once told me Hell was a really beautiful place, but I never quite believed him. How could a place where demons and wolves live be beautiful? Until this second when I'm staring at all of Hell right in front of me, I never once imagined it was like this. A giant tree has grown from below the city and its entangled roots stretched everywhere they could. I remember the tree being called The Tree of Ignis. The tree has made winding paths that swirl around the main trunk, lit up with red fire on its edges. Pack homes are also woven into the branches and roots, almost like they are part of the tree. Sharp and steep rocky mountain walls make a circle around the outskirts of the city, one of them I've just fallen down, which must have one of many portals to Hell on it.

No wonder that hurt like a bitch. The fall must be about thirty feet.

I didn't even know there was a portal to Stormfire near my home. In fact, it should be impossible for that portal to even exist. *Problem for another time.*

The Stormfire city surrounds the major part of the ancient and wondrous tree. The looping roots and gnarled vines hold much of the city together. There are tall towers of apartments wrapped in vines and red flowers, that are like flames, on the edges of the city. Closer to the middle are large stone buildings that seem untouched by the tree themselves, and perhaps newer.

The tree isn't the most beautiful and fascinating part of the city.

No, it's the leaves.

Burning leaves constantly fall off the branches at the top of the tree. They flutter down and then disappear into nothing but embers before they hit the ground. I stare around in awe at the place I've always wanted to come to see.

Terrified awe.

What the hell am I going to do? I bite my back-pack in my mouth a little tighter, wondering what Mum packed inside it for me and if she is still alive. My wolf whines softly, our pain shared between us, threatening to take over the fear we need to focus on. It isn't safe here. I glance back up at the portal at the top of the massive hill that

I've just fallen down. Rizer is going to follow me here soon. He is too powerful for me to fight head-on, and there's no way I'm going to get away from him in his pack's territory if he spots me now. I glance back at the tree and Stormfire city resting around it.

There's only really one thing I can do to survive: hide in Rizer's pack of millions of Stormfire wolves and make sure he doesn't find me.

He won't think I'm brave enough to hide in his own pack. *Hopefully.*

At least I won't stand out in Stormfire, not with my red fur wolf, as they all appear the same as me, something I've always wanted. Just not like this. Except for the white streak of hair, but I can disguise that with a hat or something in human form. Not so much as a wolf. I lean back on my heels and tighten my grip on the backpack before I break out into a run. My wolf bolts across the rocky terrain that seems like it's on fire, but it does nothing but heat my paws. In fact, I feel warm but not on fire like I should do.

"Outside the gates of Hell's city burn all those who flee and do not belong."

My academy teachers' words come back to haunt me as I keep running and come to a large river made of clear, crimson water. Sharp rocks sit at the bottom, and a few strange fish swim around them. *Let's hope none of them bite.* The current of the river flows fast, and I don't see a bridge in sight or anywhere I can cross.

We'll have to swim.

Feeling my wolf's reluctance to go into it, and I'm completely in agreement with her, I figure we don't have a choice. We're not great at swimming. It was never one of our bonus points at the academy, but there's no way around it. I pull the backpack tightly into my mouth, knowing I need to hold on firmly to it in the river.

We can do this!

I dive into the water, and my wolf uses all our strength to swim to the other side. We try not to get pushed too far down by the current, but the river is deeper and bigger than we thought. The water is warm, almost painfully warm, but I try not to focus on it as we swim as fast as we can to the other side. Soon we realise the current is much wilder than we predicted, and suddenly we are being pushed harshly around. My wolf dives underwater, and we bare our teeth, holding the backpack to push through the current. It directs our path. I know I need to let the current take me and not fight it, even as I can't see or hear anything but red water.

It's official. Hell sucks, and they even ruined water.

My wolf pulls free of the current eventually, and we break out of the top of the river, gasping for air around the backpack. We end up just being pulled and pulled farther down the river, not able to get out of the current to either side. My legs ache, and tiredness takes over with every brush of a wave of water against us. The only good thing is that Rizor is unlikely to find me now. The dreadful thing is that rivers like this can only end in two ways. One could be a pretty lake and the other a deadly waterfall.

With my luck, it is definitely going to be a waterfall.

No sooner do I think that than the rushing of a waterfall in the distance carries to my ears, and pure panic makes me struggle around in the water. I want to shift back, but I know it's not a good idea. My wolf is stronger than I am. She goes back underwater with the current, and we try swimming tougher when we come back up, but it doesn't get us anywhere. I glance around as quickly as possible, looking for anything to help us get out of this damn river. That's when I see it, a big rock ledge on the left side, next to the edge of the waterfall cliff. If I could just land on to that, I can climb out and be on the right side for the city.

I swim as hard as I can towards it, pushing my wolf to her limits, begging our body not to give our tiredness.

We really need to work on our cardio and swimming skills if we survive this.

We just about slam our body into it, my lungs gasping from the impact, and I nearly drop the backpack out of my mouth. Pulling myself up onto the ledge, I reel my weak legs across to the side of the rocky pathway and finding a hidden space between a few roots of a stray tree that will hide me for a bit.

Fucking hell, I think to myself, letting out a small, frustrated whine.

I shift back, needing to be human for a moment, and take a deep breath before breaking down in sobs as the pain of everything that has happened catches up with me. Wrapping my arms around my knees, I don't know how long I cry for. Knowing that my mum's gone, knowing my dad is most likely gone, too, and I'm the alpha's intended mate.

And he rejected me.

Being rejected by someone who you're meant to mate with is unheard of in the pack world. At least I've never heard of it. But then it's also unheard of for the Stormfire alpha to take a mate. I know he has one son whose mother he murdered, but she was never his mate. Just his breeder.

How he ever thought I could be his mate is insane to think about. I'm no alpha female and I never want to take a mate. I don't want to love someone because magic forces me to. Too many times I saw my mum resist her mating bond because her mate was an asshole.

Sorry, Dad, but you were one. RIP. Hopefully.

I grit my teeth, and my wolf lets out a growl that echoes in my chest when I think of Rizor calling me weak. *I am not weak.* Taking a deep breath, I try to control my emotions, try to push down my urge to shift back. To run and run until we get out of this world, to somewhere safe from him. But I know we need to be smarter than that right now. I don't have anywhere to go back to. The alpha of Caeli won't fight the Stormfire pack for me, which he would have to do if he protected me. Rizor will never stop until he kills me…even I don't understand what he wants with my death. I can't go straight to my brother because that's exactly where he'd think I'd go. Watching my brother is going to be his first move, no doubt. I search my brain for an answer for a long time before I come up with the perfect (ish) idea.

I look up at the falling embers that drift down around me, matching the same colour as my hair. I think of my brother's best friend who lives here in Stormfire. The boy who always smelt of burning leaves and bad decisions.

Caspian Hardling.

I met him a few times as a young teenager and I fixated on him because he was Stormfire, new, interesting, and most importantly, gorgeous. His parents let him spend two years training in Caeli Academy as part of a student exchange programme to help with peace between the four packs. Caspian is a good guy, and I can trust him. My brother said he trusted Caspian with his life, and I really have no one else to turn to here. I doubt Caspian is even going to remember me; I haven't seen him since I was thirteen and blurted out I had a big crush on his handsome eighteen-year-old ass.

I was a dork who had just discovered wine. *A bad combo.*

I have to ask him to hide me until I can come up with a plan. He's a bounty hunter, or at least I heard that he was in the bounty hunter trials last year. My brother never said if Caspian passed them, like he did, but I doubt Caspian failed. When he sets his mind on something, he always gets it in the end. He told me that himself when I was a drunk little dork.

Now I have a plan, albeit not a great one, I open the backpack and find several sets of clothes inside along with a letter. My hands shake as I open the yellow envelope and pull the parchment out. I run my fingers over my name, written in my mum's beautiful, classy handwriting. A small bracelet falls out of the envelope onto my lap, and I lift it to see it's made of silver with a red stone attached in the middle of it. I put the bracelet down and open the letter to read it.

To Lilith,

I'm so sorry that I had to write this, that I couldn't tell you everything, that you're in this position. I knew if you took this backpack that everything I feared would happen has happened. I know I'm not with you because I'd never let you read this letter if I was.

First thing's first.

The bracelet is spelled. I used all of my money over my short lifetime to pay for it, and it's blessed by demons of incredible power. It will hide you from him. The Stormfire alpha can never find or track you so long as you wear it. Neither will anybody else who will look for you and have been since you were born. The Caeli pack hid you until now, but now you have to find your place in the world alone. I'm so sorry.

Wear it and never take it off, promise me this.

There's so much I wish to tell you, so much that I can't fit into a small letter. But I'm going to sum up most of the terrible things that happened right before you were born. I was born in the Caeli pack, but I gave my heart to Storm-fire. To your father. Know that I created you in pure love, no matter what anyone says.

Many people died to keep you safe, to get me out of Hell, but it all went wrong. And at the very last second, I had to make a deal to leave Hell with you. The alpha of Stormfire wanted you as his mate. I think he always did because of what happened when you were born. Many want you as theirs, Lilith, and you must trust no one.

I can never write the truth in this letter because if someone else found this, it could mean the death of you. I wish I could have told you, but your dad bound me to the secrecy, so it could never leave my lips.

I'm sorry.

The secrets will come out eventually, and you'll realise what I did for you was the right thing, but for now the secret will die with me.

Be brave.

We both know that hiding in Hell is the best for you if you can get there. You'll fit in there as it is massive, full of millions and millions of wolves, the biggest population of wolves in the world. You'll be able to hide and disappear.

I will love you forever and I will protect you in the afterlife. Always know dying for you was my plan right from the beginning. I regret none of my life or my choices.

Tell your brother that. Let him know there is a letter for him in our secret place.

Love,

Mum

By the end of the letter I'm in sobs as I pick up the small bracelet my mum said she spent so much money on. No wonder we barely had anything and Dad hated me so much. It looks expensive, and it radiates with magic. The sort of magic that doesn't come cheap anymore. The only things in this world that have magic are demons. Demons don't sell their magic easily or cheaply or to anybody in Caeli. I clip the bracelet onto my wrist, feeling my mum's love and protection in it like she is here at my side. The stone rests right in the centre of my wrist, fitting me perfectly.

What secret would my mum die to protect about me? What could be so bad but desirable to the Stormfire alpha?

What the hell happened when I was born?

Of course, no one answers me, and I bet the secret is with the Crescent Goddess now.

I need to get to Caspian and somewhere safe because I can't die or get caught now. My mum needs me to be strong, to fight this and live my life. Rizor will tell his people to look for me, no doubt. I need to get into the city and disappear. Soon he will have the entire pack searching for a new wolf.

Quickly, I drag on the leggings, boots, and the large hoodie that's in the backpack, one of my favourite hoodies that I thought I'd lost over a year ago. *I know exactly where it went now.* I smile for a brief second at the idea of my mum stealing it.

Then my smile falls when I remember she isn't here anymore. She is likely dead.

I pull my wet hair into a ponytail with a hairband I find in the bag and drink the small bottle of water that's at the bottom before putting everything back and standing. Strapping the backpack onto my back, I glance up at the enormous city. A city big enough for any wolf to get lost in.

Time to go into the city of Hell and pretend I'm from here.

I don't know if that's even possible because I have no idea what I'm walking into. The river will have hidden my scent and washed away all traces of any Caeli wolf on me. That's one good thing. I walk towards the city walls, and when I get to them, I realise there's no door anywhere I can see. I search up and down the wall, realising I have to go through the main gates of the city.

Unless…

I look up and grimace. Maybe I can climb the wall and get into the city, even if my climbing skills might not be great. It's worth a try. Using the roots, I climb as quickly as I can despite that every few steps I almost slip. My heart pounds faster each time.

I keep climbing until I get to the top and pull myself onto my back, breathlessly staring at the roots above me. Sweat coats my forehead, and I wipe it away. Falling, burning leaves drift down from the tree above and around me. They seem so beautiful in the many lights around me, the smell of smoke and fire is relaxing even as the noise of the city drowns out the idea of silence. The wall must have blocked some sounds as it's much louder up here and reflects the noise a city of millions in it would have. The red glow is bright on my face, followed by a mixture of white light coming from the city. It almost appears like a sunset here, a sunset of so many shades of oranges, reds, and pinks. I always wanted to travel the world, but I always wanted to do it and then come back to tell my parents about the world outside of Caeli.

Now that can't happen.

With strength I didn't know I had, I slide myself over the other side of the wall and climb down the roots until I can jump to the floor. I quickly glance around me to make sure I'm safe. No one is close to me, nothing but rubbish and a dumpster that blocks anyone from seeing me. Two buildings are to my left, and I walk down the space between them and hide by the wall to peek around the corner. One massive pathway that leads right into the city is near me, and hundreds of wolves in human form stroll down them, some with small demon creatures on chains walking at their sides. So many people, and not one of them turn my way. I sneak out from behind the building, joining the crowd but keep my eyes down on the floor, and pulling my hood up to cover my hair. It doesn't take long to get closer to the middle of the city. The noise of people talking, music playing, bangs, and wolves howling fills my ears and senses when I try to break out of the crowd.

I search the buildings, reaching out with my senses for any trace of Caspian, but there are too many scents, too many wolves for me to search for him alone. It's all too much here, and a part of me likes it. The energy of the city is amazing. I come past a poster clipped to a building side and pause, seeing an advertisement for the bounty hunting trials in big bold letters.

Someone there might know where Caspian is, and it isn't a place the alpha would look for me, I don't think. At the bottom of the advertisement is a small map of Hell with a star over where the bounty hunting trials are. I rip it off and take a deep breath before setting off to find the only wolf in Hell who can help me.

CHAPTER FIVE

LILITH THORNBLOOD

"Derek, if that's you back without my fucking demon—" Caspian pauses mid-sentence, slowly dropping his deep caramel eyes down onto me.

I didn't think the tip I got from a man outside the large fenced-off area for the demon-hunting trials was right when he said Caspian lived here. Mostly because the man appeared drunk, and it was too lucky that the first person I asked actually knew Caspian at all.

Turns out the long shot was bang on.

Caspian's six-foot, built-as-hell frame towers over me. I forgot how intimidating his stare is.

"Who the fuck are you and what do you want?"

I'm speechless for a second too long. With unsee-able speed, he whips a silver dagger out from his back and places the tip under my chin. Fury burns in his eyes, and two black marks that run down from his forehead and around his eyes to his cheeks glow a vibrant red. "You might be fucking drop-dead beautiful but you won't trick me into whatever you're selling. Get the fuck out of here before you regret it."

He lowers the dagger and walks back into his house.

"I'm Leo's sister!" I shout seconds before the door shuts in my face.

But then it swiftly swings open again, and Caspian rests his shoulder against the doorframe. This time, he pauses to look at me from head to toe, and I do the same to him.

Caspian Hardling has changed since he was eighteen.

He's still as breathtakingly handsome as he was then but he is more now. So much more.

Beefy shoulders fill out his white button-down shirt, which is tucked into black leather trousers with laces at the front of his narrow but toned waist. The trousers showcase his thick thighs and other areas. His soft, silky blond hair is tipped white and falls to just below his ears. His ears are spiked at the top, a reminder of his demon blood, and I've always thought they suit him. All demons have tipped ears in human form, but it's more complicated for half-demon, half-wolves like Caspian.

He is rare. Few half-borns survive childhood.

"You grew up, songbird."

I narrow my eyes at his stupid nickname for me. The memory of it comes back like a hammer. How did I have a crush on this guy? Oh, right. Wine, teenage hormones, and one sexy-ass half-wolf.

Apparently, I sing as well as demon songbirds, which for the record, screech all night and can make human men go deaf. They are popular for torture.

"Clearly you haven't," I say, crossing my arms.

"Did you come all the way to Hell to insult me? Or did you miss my pretty face?"

Swallowing my pride, what is left of it, I tell him the truth. "Neither. I need your help because I'm in danger."

Something changes in his eyes, the playfulness disappearing as he straightens. "I can't help you. You need to go."

"Wait!" I stop his door closing in my face this time.

He sighs.

"My brother said you owed him. A life debt, if I'm not mistaken."

He arches a pierced brow. "And?"

"This will make you even. Help me, for my brother, for the debt if nothing else," I reply, hoping this will work. I'm sure Leo will go along with the plan if I had any way to safely get in touch with him.

Caspian stares down at me once more, and slowly he steps back, waving me into his house. "Get the fuck in, songbird."

"My name is Lilith, in case you've forgotten," I respond. I walk into the spacious yet empty room. There is a generic kitchen with four counters, a fridge, and a small bathroom behind a screen on the other side. A double bed is in the middle, with a couch at the end and a big orange rug in front of it. A wardrobe is near the bed, with two hooks on either side and countless weapons hanging off the large hook.

Other than that, there is nothing else here. Nothing personal to be seen.

Caspian slams the door shut behind me and walks around me to the fridge. "Do you drink yet? How old are you again?"

I drop down onto his leather sofa. "Old enough."

"Good, because we need vodka for this conversation where you blackmail me into saving you from whatever the fuck you have done."

Caspian brings over a half-drunk bottle of vodka and two shot glasses, chucking one at me. I hold it up, and he pours me a shot. I down it, keeping my eyes on him, and he raises an eyebrow at me before taking his own shot.

He downs another one and then pours himself a third. "Talk."

"My mum and dad were killed by the Stormfire alpha. He wants me dead, and I need to hide," I blurt out in one long rush.

Caspian coughs on the shot and smacks his fist against his chest a few times, staring at me with wide eyes.

"Then you're dead already. I can't help you fight him," he replies, still looking shell-shocked.

I get the impression not much surprises this guy.

Rolling my eyes, I glance away. "I know that and I need somewhere to hide in the city. Permanently."

"Does the alpha know you're here?"

"Maybe," I respond, clasping my hands together. "I don't know for sure. So can I hide here?"

"Minor problem, I'm leaving here tomorrow." He rubs the back of his neck and tilts his head at me. "The demon hunter trials begin tomorrow, and I'm joining them."

"Shit," I mutter. "Do you know anyone who could hide me? Someone you trust?"

He scoffs. "I don't trust anyone in Hell, and you shouldn't either, songbird."

He sits on the sofa next to me, only a few inches between us, and I try not to look at the gorgeous fucker who is clearly going to ditch me.

"I'm sorry about your parents. Really, I am," he eventually says. "More your mum though. Your dad was a dick."

"Technically, he wasn't my dad," I counter, trying to make light of it with some dark humour.

Caspian chuckles low. "Lucky you."

We drift into silence once more before Caspian lets out a long sigh. "I'm going fucking mad because I have an idea. It's crazy, but it just might work if you don't fuck it up."

My heart thrashes. "I'm willing to go for crazy right now."

Caspian's gaze trails over me, the marks on his cheeks almost glowing red for a second, and I wonder what that means. When he was in Caeli, his marks never glowed, and I overheard him telling Leo that they were from his father's demon side, not his wolf's.

"I could get you into the demon hunter trials under a fake name," he says slowly, "and I doubt the alpha would search for you there. The faces of all contestants are kept a secret, so they can move around the city freely. The alpha gives his protection to each of the ten winners. If you could win, which I highly doubt, by the way, you could gain the alpha's protection. Then he won't be able to kill you without breaking his vow."

"Which means death for an alpha," I whisper, filled with hope. "You're right… That is a crazy plan."

"Told you. Now the question is, can you fight? Do you know fuck all about demons?"

"Well, I know you."

He smirks and rests back, picking the vodka bottle up and taking a long drink. "That you do, songbird. That you do."

I just manage to resist snorting at him. "I don't think your plan will work, but it might buy me more time to find a safe place to escape. Somewhere the Stormfire alpha can't reach," I say and stand off the sofa. I snatch the vodka bottle from his hands and take a sip.

He grins when I scrunch my face up at the taste. "There are no demons on the moon."

Rolling my eyes, I shove the bottle back his way. "I've always wanted to be a demon hunter."

Caspian slowly moves his attention up my body, and I feel his gaze like fire against my skin until he clashes with my eyes.

"You're going to make an interesting partner, songbird."

"Thank you for helping me," I reply shakily.

He stands, stretching his long, thick arms. "Don't thank me yet. There is every chance the leader of the trials is going to take one look at you and say fuck no."

"Then I'll have to be charming," I say with a wink.

Caspian flashes me a devilish smirk. "If you can charm the alpha's only son, then I'm a fucking virgin."

He laughs, walking away from me. My cheeks burn as red as my hair. I have to get into these trials; alpha's son or not, I'm going to get in.

"By the way, we need to dye that white streak of hair. It makes you stand out," he calls back, walking to his door. "Don't go anywhere, songbird."

"Like I can!" I shout as he leaves me alone in his apartment.

What the hell, pun intended, have I gotten myself into?

DESCRIPTION

The alpha of hell is my fated mate and he rejected me.

I'm an outcast in my pack and have been since the day I was born. Shunned by most of the wolves around me, I've managed to stay out of trouble… until now.
Now The Alpha of Stormfire is hunting me, but he doesn't want to claim me as his mate.

He wants me dead.

Forced to leave my old life behind, I have no choice but to go on the run. Luckily, The Demon Hunting Trials is the perfect place to hide, even if it comes with a few obstacles.

Such as their leader is a total jerk, a wolf is

blackmailing me to be his friend, and I swear my new, sexy as sin partner is trying to get us killed.

With demons running amok and the alpha of hell searching for me, I hope I can live long enough to get my revenge.

18+ Dark reverse harem romance full with a sassy and sarcastic heroine who finds her match.

BONUS READ OF ALPHA HELL...
LILITH THORNBLOOD

*T*here isn't enough booze in the shifter world to deal with alpha egos.

I take a deep drink of the red wine I stole from the teacher's lounge at Caeli Pack Academy before passing it to my best friend. The only person in the whole world (okay, just the academy) who I like. She's also the sole reason the alpha's sons are walking right over to us at this lame excuse for a party to celebrate the rare blood moon. Who throws a party for eighteen-year-olds without booze?

Aurelia Winters coughs as she takes a long drink and rolls her eyes at me when I chuckle. Although she tends to think otherwise, Aurelia is ridiculously stunning, and it's mostly down to her bloodline. She looks just like her mum, but her father's genes are strong and make her the perfect example of a Caeli wolf. Taking another sip from the bottle, Aurelia tucks her curly blonde hair behind her ears and looks past me at the alpha's sons with her big blue eyes. She is the perfect wolf at the Caeli Pack Academy, whereas me, on the other hand, I stand out as the outcast they put up with. I'm a red in a world of white with my dark-red hair and red-furred wolf. Other than the streak of white hair that falls down the side of my cheek, there isn't much about me that lets me mix in with the pack I have always lived in.

The Caeli Pack is hidden deep in the snowy Mountains of Alaska, where no one ever comes because it's too high up and the humans are afraid of us. Mostly because we're supernatural beings who don't mix well with them since they only see us as a means to protect them from the bad things in the world. Every pack in the world has its mission, its purpose, and Caeli's is learning and recording every event in the world of shifters. Basically, librarians with a bite.

"I stand out everywhere," I mutter to Aurelia.

"So? You're pretty and unusual here. That's not a bad thing," she replies. "Don't worry so much."

Says the girl who fits into our pack better than my ass fits into these skinny jeans. I don't hide or blend in very well. Aurelia is the opposite. At least, she is until we're at a party like this where she stands out far more than I do in some sense. It's all because of the mating season. In a year's time, most females will have chosen a mate, and the males all want the prettiest wolf in the pack which is Aurelia.

Finding a mate is definitely not on my to-do list. At least not with any of these wolves.

I take the bottle from Aurelia. "I think I should just leave at the end of the academy year in two weeks. Maybe join the demon-hunting trials in the Stormfire pack or something." Throwing back a deep mouthful, I wipe my lips with the back of my hand. "Hell, maybe I could look for my father and actually fit in there."

Aurelia gawks at me, then snatches the bottle. "Are you freaking crazy? You could also die in the trials. That's it. No more booze for you."

I glare at her jokingly. "Hey, I'm not even tipsy!"

"You're speaking like my aunt on New Year's Eve! Have you forgotten that you could get killed trying to capture those disgusting demons? They eat wolves for fun. Why would you even want that?" She shakes her head. "You're safe here. You shouldn't leave."

"My brother left."

With a sigh, she rests her head on my shoulder for a few seconds. "But he's a male and strong. There are like three female demon hunters in the whole of the Stormfire pack, and each of them are totally badass."

"So you're saying I'm not a badass?" I question with a raised eyebrow.

She laughs. "If you were brought up in Stormfire, taught to fight from a kid instead of how to read a book and study like our pack taught, we might be having a different conversation. But your circumstances are totally different. You were brought up a Caeli, and we both don't have a clue about fighting demons or capturing them. Come on, Lilith. You know this. Please tell me you weren't being serious?"

I don't answer her because I know she's right. But the thought of studying wolf history and doing nothing more than studying for the rest of my life makes me feel sick. It's like my pack is squeezing the life out of me with each passing day, and the only way to stop is to find an escape.

"We can talk about it later," I say, shrugging my shoulder. "They are nearly here."

Aurelia raises her head and straightens her tight, sparkling yellow dress that shows off her long legs. I cross my own covered legs, the movement straining my jeans and knocking mud off my heavy boots. Aurelia decided that we both needed to dress up and come to this party at one of her friend's houses, something that I would never attend before now because honestly, parties are not my thing. I'd much rather be drinking this bottle of red wine on my own back in my room, but I can't always be unsociable when my best friend is a big extrovert. I need to compromise sometimes, even if that means leaving my bedroom. C'est la vie, right?

The alpha sons stomp over from the dance floor that we can see at the end of the corridor we are sitting in. The blasting music vibrates through the room, shaking the floor almost from the noise of it, and pop song comes on that sings about humans shaking their asses. Another reason I tend to avoid these things. Why does the music always suck? I'd much rather they played some rock. Hell, if they put on some Guns N' Roses, I might even bust some real moves. None of this swaying, grinding nonsense.

Beside me, a dancing Aurelia knocks my shoulder as she sings the song word for word. I can't help but smile at her. I thought I could hide back here with her, but now the alpha's twin sons' shadows hang over us, I'm thinking my hiding skills need work.

This was a really bad idea.

They're both looking at her like she's the answer to their prayers, the very air to their lungs, while their mating scent invades my own lungs so much that I nearly gag. They never stop staring at Aurelia even as they finally come to a stop, and I know why. Everyone knows she's going to be an alpha female at some point because her wolf is strong, a born leader, and her human incomparably beautiful.

All the things you need to be on the alpha's sons' radar.

As for me? Everyone knows I'm only ever going to be the outcast. It's because I really, really don't belong in this pack. Caeli is all about reputation and utmost control, of unrivalled intellect and centuries-old knowledge that are the very bones of our existence. Each pack in our world has its own unique purpose. Caeli's is record-keeping and the continuous search for better, more proficient pack medicine; something that has been installed into me since I was a pup.

Learn for the Pack—the motto every wolf here lives by.

Every wolf except for me.

As my mum puts it, I've always been too wild, too uncontrollable, and in general too nosy for my own good. I'm sure that's the sole reason most of the teachers at this academy absolutely hate me and most likely the reason that my adopted brother sometimes pretends I'm not really his sister. Being an embarrassment to the shifter world is weirdly something I can live with. But being an embarrassment to my own family is the only thing that's kept me from running away.

Damn, I need more wine if I'm going to think about my family.

The alpha's sons, Dumb and Dumber as I've nicknamed them, just gaze with wide eyes at Aurelia. Their expressions are almost panicked. Aurelia watches back and sighs. It always makes me laugh how the simple fact she stares down future alphas who will no doubt one day fight for the chance to be pack leader, and subsequently, choose her as the alpha female if she chooses them, too. But I don't know if she will. Aurelia is picky about her guys, a lot like me. Not that many have been interested in the girl who doesn't belong here. Beyond their curiosity, I'm usually too different for them to look at twice.

The alpha sons may be handsome and muscular, both of them built like dump trucks, but for as strong as they are, there's not a lot going on upstairs under their thick, white-blond hair. My point is proven when they both stumble for a second on what to say to Aurelia. They scratch their heads, no doubt in search of a cheesy, over-thought chat-up line, and then one of them says something that surprises even me a little.

"Would you like to come and dance to the song that is playing? I heard you say it was your favourite once."

And for whatever reason in the world, Aurelia appears almost happy that one of them noticed she likes the song that's playing.

She looks at me, and I nod. "Go. I'm going back to my room with the wine."

"Okay, see you back there later," she replies with a big smile.

The two of them quickly wander off down the corridor, and I hear her laugh a while later as I take another long drink of the bottle. A warm buzz floats down my body, the wine finally kicking in, but then I notice I'm left alone with the other alpha's son who I can never remember the name of. Every girl at this academy, other than me and Aurelia, has got their names memorised and written down in their diaries with love hearts. I know she doesn't do silly stuff like that just because we share a room and have done since we both came here when we were eight, like every young pack member. Their names come back to me now I gaze at them; Mathi and... Dammit, I can't remember what the other one's name is.

I stand and fake a big yawn before trying to walk away. But Mathi reaches out and grabs my arm, stopping me. I knew it was never going to be that easy. These alpha-holes rarely ever take a hint.

I narrow my eyes on his brown ones, a big contrast to my light grey. "Let. Go."

A smirk slides over his lips. "No. Why should I?"

He moves closer to me, lining up our bodies, and the disgusting thoughts circling in his head are written on his face as clear as day. This asshole better back off. He can't touch me; his father himself accepted me into the pack, which means I have the alpha's protection until he isn't alpha anymore. Of course, I worry about what will happen to me if the next alpha, AKA Dumb or his brother, Dumber, become alpha. But that won't be for some time yet. Right now, my focus is to get this unwanted paw off my body.

At the sight of me trying to wiggle my arm free, his smirk deepens into a malicious smile. He tightens his grip and pulls me closer, bringing his lips to my ear.

"You and I both know no one would notice if you went missing. You are just the outcast, the red wolf in a pack of white purebreds." He jolts me harder against him, his hands leaving bruises on my arm, but I refuse to turn away, to even wince at the pain. "Actually, that begs the question as to why you are still here. I'm surprised my father let you into the academy at all, half-breed."

Searing rage slams into me at the insult. Half-breed is the delightful nickname purebreds use for wolves like me; a subtle reminder of our so-called inferiority. Well, that's what they like to think. Anyone who's called me a half-breed usually walks away with a black eye.

I ball my hands into fists. "Maybe your dear father likes my mum a little too much. He does always seem to be admiring her."

The wolf's smile fades, and I inwardly chuckle at his stupid expression. So easily provoked, these young alphas. However, my satisfaction is short-lived. With a growl, he slams me into the wall, and I gasp from the impact. He presses his thick forearm against my neck, holding me in place, and the air dies in my lungs.

"Is that… any way… to treat a lady?" I choke out, unsure why I'm using my last breaths to anger him further. Then again, the fury burning on his gaze does make my sacrifice worth it. Besides, it's not like I'm unused to assholes like this one asserting their authority over me. Alphas love putting unruly wolves like me in their place.

Too bad I've never quite learned how to stay in mine.

Despite the black spots seeping into my vision, I stare up at him, wondering what exactly he's going to do. One thing is for sure—this dickwad has solidified my desire to leave his pack as soon as possible. I'll never follow an alpha who treats their packmates this way.

"Do you want to die, half-breed?" he growls.

I resist the urge to give him a sarcastic reply. I may be brave, but as my brother puts it, I can be pretty stupidly brave.

And I know that challenging an alpha son is really not a good idea.

I might be able to fight well, thanks to all the training the Academy has taught me. But even I know that you can't beat a guy twice your size in a small corridor like this, with no weapons on me, and his forearm pressed on my windpipe.

He gazes down at me and raises an eyebrow, but something burns on my arm.

In the corner of my eye, my wolf mark in the middle of my arm burns vividly. The swirls that form a wolf shape glow a deep, vibrant red, at first burning painfully but they quickly fade into a dull ache that fills my entire body.

Mathi follows my gaze to the mark and smiles.

"Seems like your parents are calling you home," he snarls, loosening the pressure on my throat. "Did your mum's mate ever realise that you weren't his?"

This asshole knows damn well my dad knows I'm not his. I was conceived and born before my mum ever mated. Everyone in the pack knows it. It was a big scandal, and to this day I still hear the boring wolves talking about it. Caeli wolves love to gossip because they have nothing better to do.

I grit my teeth at the jab. "Fuck. Off."

He raises his free hand as if to strike me. I don't flinch, and that seems to piss him off. He grabs me by the scruff of the neck and slams me against the wall again, drawing everyone's attention.

"Go back to your little family, half-breed. But just remember that when I'm alpha, your kind will never be welcome here." He releases me with a derisive scoff. "Off you go now, run back home."

I don't reply despite the tinge of fear that his threat elicits in me. My wolf, however, bares her teeth and snaps her jaw at him in retaliation. I need to get out of here before I shift and try to take on an alpha twice my size. The fading burn from my family's mark sears in my mind, screaming down to my soul for me to move.

Biting back my spiteful retort, I jog down the corridor and take a left out of the noisy house, dodging students who whistle and tease me. The cool night air lifts my hair over my shoulders when I step onto the porch. I take a deep breath and jog into the snowy outskirts that surround the house. Snow-capped trees line the distance, and I make a break for them. The cold doesn't bother me, even when I duck behind a tree and strip off. Once I'm fully naked, I bundle my clothes into a ball and shove them into the small bag I always carry with me.

I rest my head against the tree and gaze up at the moon cutting through the frozen leaves. My breath comes out in puffs of smoke, and for a moment I stay there, thinking about how much I'd have liked to punch that alpha-hole in the throat.

But my family needs me.

I dig my feet into the earth and arch forward, spreading my fingers through the snow. Shifting is an effortless, painless task for me, almost like breathing. I transform into my wolf easily, letting my body change until my red paws sink into the ground. Picking the bag up with my fangs, I run through the forest back towards the towering academy hidden in a clearing shrouded in blankets of untouched snow. It's eerily silent at this time of night. Most people are sleeping, and those who find themselves awake under the light of the moon, venture into the woods to hunt.

The side door of the academy is always left open, and I slip through it. The wood corridors echo every hit of my wolf's claws on them as we dodge around corridors of lockers. We keep running until we get to the main stairs and head straight up to our room and pause. My wolf drops my bag on the floor, and we use our advanced hearing to make sure no one is around before shifting back. Most wolves don't care about nudity, but I'm not one of them.

I unlock my door and head inside with my bag, quickly getting back into my jeans, plain black tee-shirt and boots. I search the messy floor for my phone next. I push a few items of clothing around before I find it and try ringing my parents, but it goes straight to voicemail. I ring my adopted elder brother, but again, straight to voicemail. My family are bloody useless with phones. Instead of trying to keep ringing them, I decide I might as well just go and see them since it's not too far to walk. It's a weird thing for them to use a wolf call with my mark, but I'm sure everything is fine, even if something in the back of my mind doesn't think so. My mum never uses the mark to summon me, and my dad definitely hasn't done it. He likes to pretend I don't exist. That only leaves my brother, but Leo's too busy working as a new demon hunter to bother summoning me. I guess there's only one way to get to the bottom of this.

Time to go home and see what the hell is going on.

Alpha Hell (The Rejected Mate Series #1)...

ABOUT G. BAILEY

G. Bailey is a USA Today and international bestselling author of books that are filled with everything from dragons to pirates. Plus, fantasy worlds and breath-taking adventures.
G. Bailey is from the very rainy U.K. where she lives with her husband, two children, three cheeky dogs and one cat who rules them all.

Please feel free say hello on here or head over to Facebook to join G. Bailey's group, Bailey's Pack! (Where you can find exclusive teasers, random giveaways and sneak peeks of new books on the way!)

Find more books by G. Bailey on Amazon... Link here.

MORE BOOKS BY G. BAILEY

HER GUARDIANS SERIES

HER FATE SERIES

PROTECTED BY DRAGONS SERIES

LOST TIME ACADEMY SERIES

THE DEMON ACADEMY SERIES

DARK ANGEL ACADEMY SERIES

SHADOWBORN ACADEMY SERIES

DARK FAE PARANORMAL PRISON SERIES

SAVED BY PIRATES SERIES

THE MARKED SERIES

JOIN BAILEY'S PACK TO CHAT WITH ME!

Join my Facebook group, <u>Bailey's Pack</u> to stay in touch with me, find out what is coming out next, exclusive teasers, and signed paperback giveaways!

STAY IN TOUCH

SIGN UP TO MY NEWSLETTER FOR FREE BOOKS,
TEASERS, GIVEAWAYS AND MORE...
SIGN UP HERE.
FOLLOW ME ON INSTAGRAM-
Instagram
FIND ME ON FACEBOOK-
Facebook
TWITTER IS ALWAYS FUN-
Twitter
WANT TO SEE THE BOARDS FULL OF MY IDEAS-
Pinterest

FIND ALL MY BOOKS HERE-

WWW.GBAILEYAUTHOR.COM

Printed in Great Britain
by Amazon